YUU
MIYAZAKI

ILLUSTRATION BY
okiura

D1255187

THE ASTERISK WAR

01. ENCOUNTER WITH
A FIERY PRINCESS

"IF I WIN, THEN I GET TO DO WHATEVER I WANT WITH YOU."

JULIS-ALEXIA VON RIESSFELD

"THIS SCHOOL'S GONNA BE A LOT TOUGHER THAN I THOUGHT..."

AYATO AMAGIRI

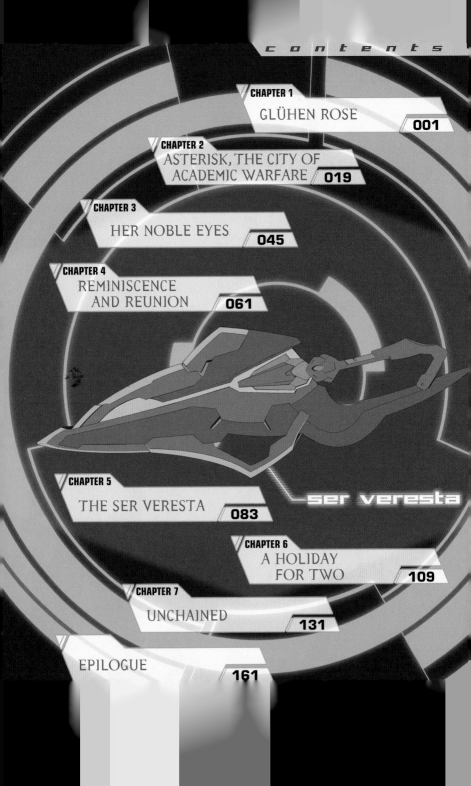

contents

ser veresta

THE ASTERISK WAR

01. ENCOUNTER WITH A FIERY PRINCESS

YUU MIYAZAKI

ILLUSTRATION: OKIURA

YEN ON

NEW YORK

RIKKA: THE ACADEMY CITY ON THE WATER

QUEENVALE ACADEMY FOR YOUNG LADIES

Their school crest is the Idol, a nameless goddess of hope. The culture here is bright and showy, and in addition to fighting ability, another criterion for admission is good looks. It is the smallest of the six schools.

COMMERCIAL AREA

MAIN STAGE

CENTRAL DISTRICT

ADMINISTRATIVE AREA

LE WOLFE BLACK INSTITUTE

Their school crest of Crossed Swords signifies military might. They have a tremendously belligerent school culture that actually encourages their students to duel. Owing to this, their relationship with Gallardworth is strained.

SEIDOUKAN ACADEMY

Their school crest is the Red Lotus, the emblem of an indomitable spirit. The school culture values individuality, and rules are fairly relaxed. Traditionally, they have many Stregas and Dantes among the students.

SAINT GALLARDWORTH ACADEMY

Their school crest is the Ring of Light, symbolizing order. Their rigid culture values discipline and loyalty above all else, and, in principle, even duels are forbidden. This puts them on poor terms with Le Wolfe.

An academic metropolis, floating atop the North Kanto mass-collision crater lake. Its overall shape is a regular hexagon, and from each vertex, a school campus protrudes like a bastion. A main avenue runs from each school straight to the center, giving rise to the nickname Asterisk.

This city is the site of the world's largest fighting event, the Festa, and is a major tourist destination.

Although Asterisk is technically a part of Japan, it is governed directly by multiple integrated enterprise foundations and has complete extraterritoriality.

OUTER RESIDENTIAL DISTRICT

JIE LONG SEVENTH INSTITUTE

Their school crest is the Yellow Dragon, the mightiest of the four gods, signifying sovereignty. Bureaucracy clashes with a laissez-faire attitude, making the school culture rather chaotic. The largest of the six schools, they incorporate a Far Eastern atmosphere into almost everything.

ALLEKANT ACADÉMIE

Their school crest is the Dark Owl, a symbol of wisdom and the messenger of Minerva. Their guiding principle is absolute meritocracy, and students are divided into research and practical classes. They are unparalleled in meteoric engineering technology.

THE ASTERISK WAR, Vol. 1
YUU MIYAZAKI

Translation by Melissa Tanaka
Cover art by okiura

This book is a work of fiction. Names, characters, places, and incidents are the product of the author's imagination or are used fictitiously. Any resemblance to actual events, locales, or persons, living or dead, is coincidental.

© Yuu Miyazaki 2012 / okiura
First published in Japan in 2012 by KADOKAWA CORPORATION. English translation rights reserved by Yen Press, LLC under the license from KADOKAWA CORPORATION, Tokyo, through TUTTLE-MORI AGENCY, INC. Tokyo.

English translation © 2016 by Yen Press, LLC

Yen Press, LLC supports the right to free expression and the value of copyright. The purpose of copyright is to encourage writers and artists to produce the creative works that enrich our culture.

The scanning, uploading, and distribution of this book without permission is a theft of the author's intellectual property. If you would like permission to use material from the book (other than for review purposes), please contact the publisher. Thank you for your support of the author's rights.

Yen On
1290 Avenue of the Americas
New York, NY 10104

Visit us at yenpress.com
facebook.com/yenpress
twitter.com/yenpress
yenpress.tumblr.com

First Yen On Edition: August 2016

Yen On is an imprint of Yen Press, LLC.
The Yen On name and logo are trademarks of Yen Press, LLC.

The publisher is not responsible for websites (or their content) that are not owned by the publisher.

ISBNs: 978-0-316-31527-2 (paperback)
978-0-316-39857-2 (ebook)

10 9 8 7 6 5 4 3 2 1

RRD-C

Printed in the United States of America

CHAPTER 1
GLÜHEN ROSE

Something floated down softly from above. Ayato caught it mostly out of reflex.

Gleaming brightly in the morning sunlight of early summer, it had looked for a moment like a pure white feather—but once it was in his hand, he could see it was just an ordinary handkerchief.

Judging from the cute yet clumsily stitched flower embroidery, it was probably not store-bought, but handmade. It did not feel very new, and with a closer look, he could see where it had been mended.

He could practically feel the affection its owner had for it. This handkerchief couldn't possibly have been discarded on purpose.

"Did it get caught in the wind…?" he wondered. *But from where?* As he turned to look around for the answer, he let out a self-deprecating laugh.

Ayato himself had just come to this city—to Seidoukan Academy. He had arrived a little earlier than planned and decided to take a stroll around campus to kill time. But the grounds were so vast that now he had no idea where he was. He wasn't exactly lost, since he had simply followed the promenade. Still, there was little hope of a newcomer like himself finding the handkerchief's owner.

"Oh, well. I guess I'll just take it to the office later."

He was about to meet the student council president anyway, so he could just hand it over then. With that thought, Ayato neatly folded the handkerchief and placed it in his pocket.

It was still early but a nice time to be outside. The promenade wound through lush trees full of the cheerful chirping of birds.

Surrounded by such natural beauty, it was hard to imagine that he was on an artificial island. But this was Asterisk, after all—the world-renowned Academic City. *They must pay close attention even to environmental aesthetics*, he thought.

Just then, Ayato noticed a voice with a hint of dismay that carried from beyond the very trees he was admiring. It rang out like a bell, no less lovely than the birdsong, but conveyed a vividly forceful will.

"...*Argh!* Of all the times, why—why *now*!?"

But as he listened more closely, he heard a litany of foul language that could scarcely be described as lovely.

Searching for the speaker, he looked up to see a single wide-open window. It belonged to a room in a neatly kept building with classical architecture, just beyond the promenade.

"I have to chase it down before it flies away any farther!"

He could hear obvious panic in the voice descending from beyond the fluttering curtains.

"So that's it." Ayato glanced down at his pocket and then back up again toward the room. He wasn't the keenest of observers, but even for him, this particular situation was easy to grasp.

"The fourth floor... Well, there are some footholds, so it shouldn't be too hard."

Between the promenade and the building was a steel fence about six feet tall. Ayato leaped effortlessly atop it, without so much as a jogging start. He then took hold of a nearby tree branch and smoothly climbed up. Such maneuvers would be unthinkable for a normal human being. But for one of the Genestella, it was nothing at all.

"Here goes...!" His destination was even higher than the treetops, but with one more jump, he reached the windowsill from a conveniently located branch. Curling his body like a cat, he landed on his feet almost soundlessly.

"Um, sorry for barging in this way. But did you happen to drop a handkerchief...?"

From Ayato's perspective, all he did was to take the simplest course of action. The person he'd overheard seemed to be in a hurry, so he thought it would be best to return the handkerchief as quickly as possible.

He acted out of kindness, pure and simple. There was no doubt about that.

However, if one were to find fault with what he did—and there were indeed some glaring faults—two issues would immediately come to mind.

The first was that this building happened to be the girls' dormitory of the Seidoukan Academy High School.

The second was that the girl to whom this room belonged was, at this very moment, in the middle of getting dressed.

"Huh...?"

"Wha...?"

Ayato and the girl, who was just stepping into her skirt, stared at each other with matching blank looks.

The girl was about the same age as Ayato—sixteen or seventeen. Azure eyes, as pale as a sprouting bud. A sleek, shapely nose and skin like fresh snow. Her hair, flowing down to her waist, was a brilliant red hue, not dark enough to describe as crimson but too vivid to be pink. Pressed to put a name to the color, he would have to call it rose.

As a matter of fact, the girl was remarkably well put together. Ayato was not the only person who would have been captivated at the first sight of her.

At that moment, the girl happened to be half naked. Her uniform blouse was unbuttoned, revealing her underthings, and she was bent over in a way that exposed the shape of her breasts to full view.

Her curves there were rather modest, but her body was unmistakably feminine, with a waist so slender it looked fragile. Her healthy, supple legs were trim all the way down to her toes, and a glimpse of adorable white panties peeked from between her dazzling thighs.

Her awkward state of dishabille made the sight far more enticing than if she had been simply naked.

For a while, the two did not move, as if frozen stiff. Considering that the girl was on one leg the whole time, she must have been blessed with an extraordinary sense of balance.

The scene looked exactly as if time had stopped. Of course, this was not the case.

Ayato was the first to come to his senses.

"S-sorry! Um, uh— I really didn't mean to—at all—!" He tried to explain himself, but the words just wouldn't come out right. He tried to cover his eyes, but between his fingers, he could still see her alluring figure.

"Wh-wh-wha—!?" The girl, too, seemed to finally comprehend the situation. Her face flushed bright red and her mouth moved without quite forming words.

Humiliation? Anger? Both? Whatever she might be feeling, Ayato was steeling himself for either a shriek or an outpouring of invective. Instead, hurrying to cover herself, the girl drew a deep breath and glared at him hard, even as tears welled up in the corners of her eyes.

"T-turn around!" she ordered in a low voice, full of forcibly suppressed emotion.

"Huh?"

"Just turn around already!"

He rushed to obey, the authority in her tone beyond question.

From behind him came the faint rustling of her clothes. And a strangely pleasant scent. Ayato could not have been more uncomfortable.

On top of that, he was still perched on the windowsill. He was one wrong move away from a deadly fall. He waited like this for several minutes, while the wind on several occasions threatened his balance.

At last she sighed and said, "O-okay. You can turn around now."

When he did so, he saw now a girl blooming with radiance.

Wearing her uniform impeccably, she cut the very picture of class and elegance—such a stark contrast to her earlier appearance that he wondered if he'd imagined it. Her sullen expression and fierce glare loudly declared a foul mood, but even that seemed somehow endearing. Ayato couldn't help but gaze at her.

She bluntly interrupted his trance. "So, the handkerchief?"

"...Sorry?"

"You were saying something earlier. About a handkerchief."

"Oh—oh yeah! Um, here it is..." Ayato took the handkerchief from his pocket and held it out to her. "I found it floating along in the wind and picked it up. Is it yours, by any chance?"

The girl inhaled sharply, opened her eyes wide for a split second, then let out a deep sigh of relief. "Thank goodness..."

She took the handkerchief and gently held it to her chest.

"Thank you. This handkerchief...it's very special to me."

"Oh no, I mean, I just happened to find it..."

"All the same. I really do appreciate it."

As Ayato stood embarrassed by her gratitude, she bent forward in a deep, formal bow. But then—

"Well, then... That's settled, I'd say," she muttered, her head still bent low. Her voice had completely changed, simmering with an emotion that might detonate at any second.

"Huh?"

The girl slowly looked up at him, a grin illuminating her face. There was, however, not a hint of mirth in her eyes. Even as her mouth made the arc of a warm smile, he noticed the corners of her lips twitching.

"Now, you die."

In the next moment, the air in the room changed completely. The girl's prana heightened explosively, and the atmosphere rumbled in response. Mana, given direction, converted the elements in the air and set a phenomenon into motion.

That aura! he thought. *Is she...?*

"Burst into bloom—*Amaryllis!*"

That instant, an enormous fireball materialized in front of the girl and flew toward Ayato.

"A Strega!?"

He pushed off backward from the window, regained his balance midair, and landed.

A deafening roar rang across the grounds in his wake. Ayato looked up to see a huge flower made of fire opening its bud to bloom—a giant wheel of flames, overlapping petals of scorching heat.

The air wavered and gusts of hot wind blew over him. It was an incredible force, exactly as if a bomb had gone off.

"...Aw, no..."

As Ayato stared in awe amid the falling sparks, the girl leaped out of the open window. Just as he had done, she landed four stories down with effortless grace.

She had to be a Genestella—one of those gifted with an affinity for mana that bestowed wondrous physical abilities. And judging by the power she had just displayed, she had to be Strega—a special class even among the Genestella.

Most of the students in the six schools of Asterisk, of which Seidoukan Academy was one, were Genestella. Even Ayato, who had little interest in the Festa, knew that much. He also knew that Stregas and Dantes, who could bend the laws of nature by linking themselves with mana, were not commonly found.

According to the theory he'd heard, even among the Genestella only a few percent manifested the talents of a Strega or Dante. And while they were gradually increasing in number, Genestella made up a very small fraction of the population to begin with. So it would go without saying that Stregas and Dantes were exceptionally rare. Ayato himself had only met one Strega in his life—before this.

"Oh... So you managed to dodge that. Not bad." The girl sounded slightly impressed, though her voice still dripped with anger. "Very well, then. I'll give you a real fight. For a bit."

"Whoa—hold on, okay!"

"What now? Just don't give me any more trouble, and I'll be nice and turn off the grill when you're well-done."

"...You mean, you want to cook me all the way through?" said

Ayato. That didn't sound at all like being nice. "Wait—I'd at least like to know why you're trying to kill me..."

"You peeped on a young lady getting dressed. It's only natural that you should pay with your life." She issued this disturbing proclamation with perfect sangfroid.

"But then, why did you thank me just now?"

"I do appreciate that you returned my handkerchief, of course. That, however, has nothing to do with this."

"...Maybe you could be a little more flexible?"

She rejected his plea with a smile. "Unfortunately, I hate that word—'flexible'!"

There was no getting through to this girl.

"Anyway, if you wanted to give me the handkerchief," she went on, "there was hardly any need to barge in through the window! Degenerates like you who sneak into the girls' dorm deserve to be beaten by an angry mob."

"Huh? The girls' dorm?" Completely dumbfounded, Ayato stared alternately at the girl and then the building. A bead of sweat trickled down from his temple.

"You mean...you didn't know?"

"How could I? I just transferred in. I'm supposed to start today. I only got here a little while ago. It's true, I swear!" As Ayato pleaded his case, he pointed to his crisp new uniform. Having hardly been worn, the jacket and pants still looked stiff.

The girl spent a few moments staring suspiciously at him, then let out a long sigh.

"Very well. I believe you."

Hearing that, Ayato exhaled in relief and put his hand to his heart.

But then, without pausing, the girl continued, "However, that still has no bearing on this."

As she smiled, more fireballs had already taken shape around her. Smaller than the one before—but this time there were nine.

"Burst into bloom—*Primrose!*"

"Ack—!"

Nine fireballs resembling graceful primroses flew at Ayato on nine different trajectories.

He contorted himself to dodge them. Some of the fireballs hit the ground, bursting with dull popping sounds and taking large chunks out of the sett-styled concrete paving. They may have been less stunningly powerful than the earlier explosion, but these were plenty lethal.

Genestella were much tougher than ordinary humans. By focusing their prana, they could defend themselves against bullets of light without any armor. Still, a direct hit from one of these fireballs would do more than tickle.

The remaining fireballs pursued Ayato from all directions. Shouting in alarm, Ayato evaded each one by a hair's breadth. He could just barely elude them by leaping in one moment and ducking down in the next.

As she watched his maneuvers, the girl's eyes widened again. "I see... You're not just a normal pervert."

Hearing an unmistakable note of praise in her voice, Ayato wiped his forehead. *Maybe she's changing her mind about me. Maybe I can get out of this alive after all.*

"You're one remarkable pervert."

Or maybe not. "Why is it so hard for people to understand each other...," he grumbled, thinking aloud.

"Hmph. That last bit was a joke." Glaring at him with narrowed eyes, she tossed her hair with a flick of her wrist. "It does appear to be true that you delivered the handkerchief out of goodwill, and I'm also willing to believe, for now, that you didn't mean to...to peep at me, um, changing... But *only* for now!"

"...Really?" Ayato couldn't help but be cautious after already getting his hopes up several times in vain.

The girl nodded reluctantly and went on. "But it *is* your fault that you didn't make sure what the building was first. And barging in by the window—that lacks any semblance of common sense. You do see, don't you, that just because you didn't do it on purpose doesn't mean that you weren't wrong?"

"Yeah… You're right." He had no argument against her logic.

"You have your defense, and I still need to quench my anger. So, I suggest that we settle this according to the rules of our fair city. Fortunately, you seem to have the skills for it. No objections, I trust?" The girl gazed straight at him. "What's your name?"

"…Ayato Amagiri."

"Mm-hmm. I'm Julis. Julis-Alexia von Riessfeld, ranked fifth at Seidoukan Academy."

Having named herself thusly, Julis lifted her right hand to her chest and touched the school crest there—the Red Lotus crest of Seidoukan Academy.

"In the name of the unyielding Red Lotus, I, Julis-Alexia von Riessfeld, challenge thee, Ayato Amagiri, to a duel!"

"A duel!?" Indifferent to Ayato's shock, the crest on his uniform shone red in response to her words. It was demanding his answer to the challenge—to accept or to decline.

"If you win, I'll accept your defense and leave you be. But if I win, then I get to do whatever I want with you." Julis smirked, as if to add, "*obviously.*"

"W-wait a second, I—"

"You transferred to this school. You must at least know about duels?"

There was no dodging the question. "…Sure, I've heard a little bit."

It would be entirely fair to say that all the students living in Asterisk were gathered there for the sole purpose of fighting. Asterisk was the site of the Festa, the largest battle-entertainment event in the world, and the students of each school were candidates to be its contestants.

"Then accept already. See, people are here to watch."

Ayato looked to see a ring of students forming around the two of them. They must have come to see what the commotion was. Most of the spectators were girls, probably because they were on the grounds of the girls' dormitory, but there were also a few boys looking on.

"Oooh, what's going on?"

"The Witch of the Resplendent Flames—the *Glühen Rose*—is dueling!"

"For real? She's a Page One! Couldn't pay me to miss this!"

"So, who's the lucky opponent?"

"Dunno. He's nobody I've seen before... Did you check the Net?"

"I *am* checking... But he's not listed in the Named Chart."

"Unlisted, huh? This guy has some stones on him."

"How long can he last? The Princess isn't the type to hold back. Like, at all."

"I give him three minutes."

"One minute."

"Hold on, the odds are coming up on the Net now. Let's see...double for three minutes or less."

"There are bookies on this already? How do they always get their intel so fast?"

"Some news clubs are broadcasting it live now. See, right there? And over there, too."

Listening to the crowd, Ayato scowled uncomfortably. There were few things he liked less than to be the center of attention. "Why is everyone staring at us...?"

"Two reasons. The first is that they want to collect data on a top-ranking student—which would be me. I'm a Page One at this school, and there's no shortage of students who'd like to take my place."

"Page One?"

"You really need everything explained to you?" Julis gave Ayato a skeptical glare. "Fine. You know that each school in Asterisk has a ranking system, right? The exact criteria differ from school to school, but each one has a list of the best fighters—the Named Chart. It contains seventy-two names in all. The top twelve on the list are called Page One, because their names appear on the first page."

That makes sense, Ayato thought.

"Now, reason number two is quite simple: These people are all idiots starving for things to gawp at."

...Right.

"Of course, if you really don't feel up to it, I can't force you. You do have the right to decline the challenge. But in that case, I'll have to hand you over to the dormitory watch. Although I *was* hoping to deal with this myself..."

Ayato was completely cornered.

But he would try one last time to talk his way out of it. "Oh, but look, I don't even have a weapon."

Some students brought their own weapons, but most would customize the equipment provided to them by the school. Ayato had been planning to do just that, if the need arose, so he didn't have a weapon yet.

"You're no Dante. What's your weapon of choice?"

"...The sword."

"Is there anyone here who can lend their weapon? A sword!" Julis called to the crowd, and the reply came immediately.

"Here ya go. Use this!" With those words, a spectator tossed something to Ayato.

Catching it, he saw that it was a device shaped like a short baton, the perfect size to hold in one hand. Embedded at one end was a green ore—manadite. He was holding a Lux activator.

"And if you don't even know how to use that, I don't want to hear it," Julis said with an audacious grin.

Ayato let out a long sigh and started up the Lux in his hand.

An angular mechanical hand guard materialized from thin air, reconstructed from the elemental pattern encoded in the manadite. The Lux shifted from standby to active mode, and a bright blade of concentrated, stabilized mana extended forth.

The blade was roughly a yard long. A fairly standard Lux with little if any modification.

Seeing this, Julis drew her own activator and switched on her Lux. Quite unlike Ayato's, it took the form of a thin, lithe rapier made of light.

"Now then, shall we begin?"

Julis fixed her eyes on Ayato as she gracefully took a stance with her slender blade.

Lux weapons were too light for him. He would have preferred a sword with some actual heft to it, but this was no time to be picky.

Holding his hand to the school crest on his chest, he mumbled out the words under a sigh. "I, Ayato Amagiri, accept thy challenge, Julis." The crest glowed bright red, confirming his will to engage.

*

The Festa was an all-style fighting event boasting the largest fan base in the world, taking place each year in the artificial island city on the crater lake left by the North Kanto mass collision—the city of Rikka, better known as Asterisk. The event was a violent spectacle, in which students from the six schools of Asterisk vied for supremacy with weapons in hand. That said, the contestants did not technically fight to kill.

The rules were spelled out in a document known as the Stella Carta. Simply put, victory was awarded to the fighter who destroyed their opponent's school crest. Although willful cruelty was forbidden, attacks on targets other than the crest were permitted if the intent was to reduce the opponent's strength. These were armed fights, so of course injuries were not uncommon—and sometimes casualties.

And yet there was a reason why young people from the world over would flock to this city. Each one came with a wish that could be granted nowhere else.

The Festa was not the only opportunity for students to fight one another. Having so many bold young people gathered in one place and eager to test their strength was bound to lead to some trouble. With such cases in mind, the laws of Asterisk allowed for personal battles to be fought.

Which was to say—duels.

Just as in the Festa, victory was achieved by destroying the opponent's school crest. However, the fortified crests were equipped with processing power, capable of judging the outcome of duels as well as forwarding the battle data to a central host computer. The intent of these measures was to prevent fraud as much as possible.

In particular, duels among students of the same school affected the rankings and therefore held significance beyond simply settling personal disputes.

Julis herself had attained the fifth rank by emerging victorious from a number of duels. But even she was puzzled by the boy who stood in front of her at this moment—this Ayato Amagiri. She couldn't read what his real strength might be.

"Burst into bloom—*Longiflorum!*"

Julis waved her blade like a conductor's baton and a spear of bluish-white flame materialized along its path. The flame, shaped like an Easter lily, shot straight for Ayato with the force of a rocket.

"*Ngh—!*" He was barely able to deflect the attack with his sword, but the impact sent him flying. He broke his fall but was already breathing hard.

"Huh. The new guy's got some chops."

"Pretty impressive, defending against the Princess's flames like that. But it looks like he's just scraping by."

"Yeah, I mean, he looks okay..."

"Not bad. But not that good, either."

"Doesn't it look like the Princess is holding back?"

Julis's shapely brows drew together as she heard the crowd's gossip. She was *not* holding back. She wasn't going all out, either, but she was taking her opponent seriously.

And indeed, no matter how one looked at it, Julis had the advantage. Ayato was completely on the defensive and couldn't even get close. Her usual tactic was to suppress her enemy from a distance with overwhelming firepower, so the fight was progressing ideally for her. She had her blade, Aspera Spina, to hold her opponent in check if they managed to close the distance.

...Right now, though, Julis couldn't shake the feeling that something was off. She couldn't quite say what it was. There was just something weird about this fight.

True, she seemed to be winning, but somehow it felt like she was attacking thin air. Ayato was evading all of her moves, if only by the narrowest of margins. For a moment, the thought crossed her mind that Ayato was the one holding back—but from the way his shoulders heaved with each breath, he certainly didn't appear to be putting on an act.

She was suspicious, but at the same time intrigued.

Studying Ayato anew, she noticed that his face, still retaining a child-like innocence, was not unattractive. He had a slim build, but it was obvious from the way he handled himself that he was in excellent shape. His dark eyes had a soft look, even in the midst of battle, making him seem somehow distant, removed. Or even, one might say, easygoing.

"Um...Miss...Julis? Maybe you could forgive me now?" Finally catching his breath, Ayato let his face relax and raised both his arms.

"Just call me Julis. So am I to take that as a gesture of surrender?"

"Sure! I mean, I never wanted to fight in the first place."

"Well, that's just fine with me. But in that case, as a pervert, you'll be either slow-roasted by me or handed over to the dormitory watch. What'll it be? Oh, by the way, I heard that the panty thief who got caught by the watch the other day was left fairly traumatized. He only speaks in broken sentences now and can't get himself to step out of his room."

"...I guess I'll try to hold out a little longer." Forcing a taut smile, Ayato once more readied his sword.

That's better, Julis thought. *I can't let this fight end before I get to the bottom of it. I have to find out what this strange feeling is.* With that determination, Julis focused her prana.

Prana was the source of a Genestella's power. It clung like an invisible aura and could be focused to heighten offensive or defensive power. For a Dante or Strega like Julis, it would also become the energy needed to activate their abilities.

Because Dantes and Stregas had to allocate prana to their abilities, they had less to use for defense and tended to be at a disadvantage in close combat.

Which was not a problem so long as she didn't let an opponent get close.

"Burst into bloom—*Amaryllis!*"

I won't miss this time. As a giant fireball emerged in front of Julis, the crowd shifted.

"Holy crap! That's her big move!"

"She's not messing around!"

"Evacuate! Evacuate!"

Spectators were responsible for their own safety. The crowd scattered in a panic.

Not even sparing a glance for the rubberneckers, Julis calculated the ideal trajectory in an instant and flung her fireball. Ayato crouched to balance himself, but just as he was about to dodge the attack, Julis clenched her fist.

"Explode!"

On her command, the fireball burst before Ayato's eyes.

Even if she couldn't land a direct hit, at that distance it was impossible to completely dodge this attack. Genestella or not, anyone swept up in an explosion at such close range would be left immobile.

Her field of vision was filled by the raging flames. As she shielded her face from the blast, Julis was convinced of her victory.

But then—

"Amagiri Shinmei Sword Style, First Technique—*Twin Serpents!*"

Julis thought she saw something gleam, like the flash of a blade, and two crossed slices quartered the petal-shaped flames.

"Wha…? Is that—Meteor Art?"

Meteor Arts were techniques to temporarily boost Lux output by pouring one's prana into the manadite. The technical term for the phenomenon was "mana excitation overload," and it was hardly the sort of thing one could learn overnight. The appropriate training was essential, not to mention intricate customization of one's Lux.

If he really did that with a Lux he borrowed only moments ago…

Julis began to feel something akin to trepidation—and then a black shadow emerged from behind the flames and closed the distance to her before she drew her next breath.

By the time she recognized the shadow as Ayato, he was already inside of her guard. His speed was beyond belief. At the very least, it was on a completely different level from his movements just a minute ago.

For a moment, she thought she saw faint sparks of light around Ayato's body. But this was no time to be distracted.

"Why, you—!" Acting on reflex, Julis moved to counter, but Ayato struck her instead with a sharp cry.

"Get down!"

Before she could process his words, she was knocked to the ground. And then Ayato's face was so close to hers, she could feel his breath. It sent a jolt through her chest. The light in his eyes was so earnest, as if he were a different person entirely.

"Wh-what are you…!?" As she tried to raise her voice in protest, her eyes went round.

A single shimmering arrow pierced the spot where Julis had just been standing. It had no solid form—it had to be Lux generated. Lux weapons created blades or bullets of light using concentrated, stabilized mana. A weapon such as a sword, wielded within the user's effective range, could be maintained for a time, but fired projectiles did not last long. The arrow disintegrated into motes of light before their eyes.

"What's the meaning of this?" The arrow had been clearly meant for Julis. The assassin must have meant it as a sneak attack in the midst of that explosion. Wherever it had come from, with timing like that, no one would have noticed. She hated to admit it, but if not for Ayato saving her, the attack would have been perfectly executed.

"The meaning of…? Don't ask me," Ayato replied, flustered. "Ask whoever just tried to shoot you."

"Not that! Why did you go out of your way to—?" Julis got that far into the sentence before she realized that someone was giving a firm squeeze to one of her still-developing breasts.

Well, not *someone*. Ayato was the one currently on top of Julis, as if in a romantic embrace, so it naturally followed that the owner of the hand was also Ayato.

As soon as Julis understood this, her face flushed scarlet.

"Oh…" Ayato, belatedly making sense of the situation, jumped off her in a panic and ducked his head in shame. "S-sorry! Um, uh— I really didn't mean to—at all—!"

Déjà vu all over again.

"Whoa! Did you see that asshole? He just jumped the Princess!"

Someone wolf whistled. "There's a ballsy move!"

"Ooh, what a passionate advance!"

The crowd, which had returned at some point, was working them-selves into a frenzy. This only served to pour oil on Julis's fiery rage.

"Wh-wh-why, you…!" In response to her fury, the air around her erupted in flames. Her anger was making her lose control of her prana.

Dumbstruck by her ferocious power, Ayato could only shake his head in denial. And then—

"All right. That's quite enough." A profoundly serene voice rang out across the grounds, along with the crisp sound of clapping hands.

CHAPTER 2
ASTERISK, THE CITY OF ACADEMIC WARFARE

"While Seidoukan Academy does recognize our students' right to hold their own duels, I'm afraid that I must nullify this one." A girl with blinding platinum-blond hair emerged from the crowd.

She was beautiful in a calm, mellow way—quite different from Julis. If Julis had the lush, radiant beauty of a rose in full bloom, this girl's beauty was deep and tranquil like a quiet lake. This, perhaps, was why she seemed much more mature than Julis even though they were likely about the same age.

"Claudia. Exactly what gives you the authority to interfere?" Julis demanded.

"Why, Julis—that would be my authority as the president of the Seidoukan Academy Student Council, of course." The girl called Claudia smiled sweetly and placed her hand on her school crest. "By the power vested in me as the representative of the Red Lotus, I hereby declare this duel between Julis-Alexia von Riessfeld and Ayato Amagiri null and void." The school crests of Julis and Ayato, glowing red until that moment, faded back to normal.

"Now you're safe, Mr. Amagiri," Claudia added with a friendly laugh.

"Whew..." So I'm really, finally out of harm's way. Ayato brushed the sweat from his forehead and breathed a deep sigh. "Thank you... uh, Miss President...?"

"That's right. Claudia Enfield, president of the Seidoukan Academy Student Council. Pleased to make your acquaintance."

She gently proffered her hand, and Ayato hurried to shake it.

Up close, he could see that Claudia was stunning in the way that made one want to stare. But her most eye-catching feature was the ample chest that strained the cut of her school uniform. Those curves were generous enough to inspire awe. It would not have been very tactful to point out, but Julis could not hold a candle to Claudia in that department.

Julis, meanwhile, appeared to be less than satisfied with the recent judgment call and had fixed Claudia with a withering glare. "I don't believe even the student council president can intervene in a duel without a valid reason."

"Oh, but there is a reason. You are aware that he's a new transfer student, aren't you? His data has already been entered into the system, so his crest judged him eligible to duel. However, there are a few more technicalities to take care of before his transferal is complete. Which means, strictly speaking, Ayato Amagiri is not yet a student at Seidoukan Academy," Claudia explained smoothly without breaking her smile. "Duels are only permitted when both parties are enrolled students. And therefore this duel is invalid. That all makes perfect sense, I think?"

Julis made a small sound of frustration and bit her lip. Going by the fact that she made no retort, she appeared to understand who was in the right.

"Well, now that we have that cleared up... Everyone, please be on your way. You wouldn't want to be late for class." At Claudia's urging, the crowd dispersed. Some were disappointed with the duel's inconclusive conclusion, but apparently not enough to complain to the student council president.

"Oh!" Ayato cried, remembering the arrow. The assassin who targeted Julis could have been among the onlookers. He might not have a full grasp of the school rules yet, but a foul attack like that had to be breaking them.

What if we're letting the culprit get away? he thought. "Um—wait, just a—"

As Ayato began to raise his voice, Julis grabbed his shoulder. "Let it go. Whoever it was is long gone." She shook her head with a cynical smile. "Besides, it's not that unusual for a Page One student to be targeted."

"She's right," Claudia agreed. "Unfortunately, incidents like that are not uncommon. Still, that was going too far. It's beyond the pale for a third party to ambush a student engaged in a duel. I'll have the disciplinary committee launch an investigation. As soon as the responsible party is identified, they will be severely punished."

Ayato was a bit taken aback by Claudia's implication that she had seen the arrow as well. There had been more than a few students in the crowd, but he doubted that anyone else among them had noticed the shot. If Claudia could see that attack in the midst of a fiery explosion, then she, too, was no ordinary student.

"Anyway, um, th-thank you…for that," Julis blurted suddenly, turning to Ayato with an embarrassed look. By "that," she had to mean Ayato saving her from the arrow.

"Oh no—it was nothing…but…"

It had all happened so quickly that in the moment, he'd had no other choice. Still, it was true—he'd tackled her to the ground, and even if it was unintentional, there was no denying that he'd touched her in an inexcusable way.

That unexpected softness under his hand was on his mind as he asked her timidly, "…You're not angry at me anymore?"

Julis, for her part, averted her eyes as a slight blush lit her cheeks. "Well, I—I can't say I'm not angry, but…you did save me."

She really is the fair and just type, Ayato thought.

Although she didn't quite look ready to forgive him, she nodded firmly. "Even I can understand that it was a force majeure situation."

This was really nothing like the handkerchief incident. Ayato had just enough time to act—not to think about it. Prana could heighten the body's physical defenses, but it wasn't enough to protect against a sniper attack.

"So, let's just say that I owe you a debt," Julis told him.

"A debt?"

"Yes. Simple enough, isn't it?"

A debt certainly was simple enough to understand, but it felt a little impersonal to Ayato.

"You really never change, do you?" said Claudia with mild exasperation. "I think your life might be easier if you were a little more honest with your feelings."

"Mind your own business," Julis retorted. "I'm honest enough as I am, and my life is perfectly fine."

"Oh, then your search for a tag team partner must be going smoothly?"

"Um... Well..." Julis awkwardly lowered her gaze. She didn't want to say any more, but she was too easy to read.

"The Festa entry deadline is in two weeks. You don't have all that much time."

"I—I know that! I'll *find* someone!" Julis whirled, her shoulders tight with anger, and headed back to the dormitory.

"Oh, dear." Claudia followed Julis with her eyes like a mother watching a petulant child stalk away.

*

"*Ahem*, so in that sense, we could say that the previous century was an era of unmitigated disaster. But the meteor shower known as the Invertia in particular caused great harm to the entire world on an unprecedented scale. Meteorites rained down for three days and three nights, forcing the world into upheaval. Considering the deterioration of existing nation-states and the rise of integrated enterprise foundations; the subsequent changes in ethical values; the emergence of a new race of human beings, born from the mana carried to Earth by the meteorites—that is, those like you, the Genestella; the field of meteoric engineering, which developed out of mana research, and the resulting explosion in technological advancement; and so on... We must conclude that for better or worse, the Invertia was a single event that completely altered the course of human history."

Walking down the hallway, Ayato could hear an elderly teacher lecturing his class.

"The mainstream view, according to the most recent academic theories, is that the Invertia did not consist of ordinary meteors. No astronomical observatories detected the shower in advance, nor were the aerosols that should have been generated on impact observed. Now, what this means is that..."

Even a minute of listening to the teacher's slow, monotonous voice was a powerful soporific. Peeking into the classroom, Ayato was not surprised to see that more than half of the students were slumped over their desks.

"You have classes this early, ma'am? Even before homeroom?"

"Yes. Although that one is a remedial class."

"A remedial class first thing in the morning..." This was going to be rough.

"Well, after all, our school philosophy values the might of both pen and sword. I do hope you take it to heart." As she led the way to the student council room, Claudia turned back to give Ayato a soft smile.

Unlike the girls' dormitory with its classical facade, the main buildings of Seidoukan Academy were modern high-rises with an open-air feeling. Three buildings—college, high school, and middle school—surrounded a spacious central quad. The high school, having the largest student body, occupied the largest building.

"Oh, by the way... You and I are in the same year, Ayato, so you should feel free to speak to me more casually."

"Huh? Miss Enfield, you're a first-year student, too?" It was hard to believe, given her calm demeanor. "Wait. If you're the student council president, then..."

It was June now. The school year began in April, so if she was a first-year student like Ayato, it had only been two months since she began high school. Ayato was not entirely clear on the process of selecting a student council president, but he would imagine it was difficult for someone to attain that office in such a short time.

"Oh, I've been president since I was in middle school. This is my third year in office," Claudia said as if it were nothing, while they walked down a glass-walled corridor brilliant with sunlight.

According to her, the student government was not divided up into middle school, high school, and college councils, but rather consisted of one student council that oversaw the entire academy, consisting of students from all levels.

"I see..."

"So please, just call me by my name."

"Okay. Got it, Miss Claudia."

"Just Claudia will do."

"But we only just met..." With Julis, they seemed to have skipped right past formalities, but normally Ayato had a hard time being so casual with a girl who had introduced herself just minutes ago.

"It's Claudia."

"But, um..."

"Clau-di-a."

"All right... Claudia."

She was much more forceful than she looked. Once Ayato gave in and called her as she'd asked, she smiled with her eyes.

"Then you'll have to just call me Ayato, too. Or it'll feel weird."

"Very well, Ayato."

"You don't have to keep speaking so formally..."

"Oh, no... This is simply a habit of mine. Please pay it no mind."

"A habit?"

"Yes. I'm actually quite blackhearted, so I always endeavor to at least present myself as polite and affable. And now I can't speak any other way."

Claudia smiled as sweetly as a doting mother, which didn't match up at all with her words, so it took Ayato a few moments to grasp them.

"...Blackhearted?"

"Oh, like you wouldn't believe. My heart is at least as black as a piece of dark matter…stewed, charred, jammed into a black hole, and topped with blackstrap molasses."

That does sound awfully black, thought Ayato.

"Would you like to see?"

"Huh?"

No sooner had she posed her question than she began to pull up her blouse.

"Hey! Wait, what're you—?"

Claudia exposed her gleaming pale midriff, and Ayato averted his eyes. Obviously, what she'd been describing about herself wouldn't be *visible*.

"Just kidding. What an adorable reaction I got out of you." Claudia playfully covered her mouth as she laughed. Ayato had totally fallen for it.

"…Here we are. Please, go on in."

They had arrived at the student council room on the top floor of the high school building. In fact, all the rooms on this floor had something to do with the student council.

The security system read Claudia's school crest, and the door opened. The room inside, however, did not appear to contain anything very relevant to student government.

A set of leather lounge furniture sat on a sepia carpet. The walls were adorned with painted views of the campus from a distance. The window was so enormous it seemed like a piece of sky, and in front of it was a heavy wooden desk. This place could have been the office of a giant corporation's CEO.

Claudia took her seat behind the desk as if she were quite accustomed to it, then clasped her fingers and let out a deep breath.

"Now, let's do this properly… Welcome to Seidoukan Academy, Ayato. I hope you enjoy your time here." She gazed intently at Ayato for a few moments, then spun her chair around and turned her eyes to the scene outside the window. "And…welcome to Asterisk."

Following her gaze, Ayato looked down at the metropolis spread out below with its orderly, perfectly shaped streets. The artificial city, floating atop an enormous crater lake, consisted of a central urban area in the shape of a regular hexagon and the six schools that protruded from each vertex like the bastions of an old fortress. Overall, the city's shape resembled that of a snowflake, which must have given the place its official name: Rikka, an old poetic word in Japanese that described snowflakes as six-petaled flowers.

A broad avenue ran from each school, meeting in the center, to the school on the opposite corner of the hexagon—the lines forming an asterisk. This became the more popularized name, perhaps because the meaning of the Japanese word was not immediately apparent to the highly international student body.

"You transferred here on a special scholarship, and we at Seidoukan Academy have only one hope for you: victory." Claudia kept her gaze on the city while she spoke. "Beat Gallardworth, best Allekant, drive out Jie Long, overpower Le Wolfe, and defeat Queenvale. That is—win the Festa. If you do, then our institution will grant whatever wish you might have. Any wish at all within the realm of earthly possibility."

"Umm…" At a loss, Ayato scratched his head and knit his brows. "I'm sorry, but that's not really what I'm interested in."

The school—or rather, the integrated enterprise foundations that stood behind each school—truly did have that power. The might of the IEFs far surpassed that of nations, which were now little more than lines on a map, and the rule of law bent easily before them. Money, power, fame, as much as one could wish for, would be ripe for the taking.

It would be fair to say that roughly half of the students gathered in Asterisk were here to pursue such dreams. As for the other half—they were Genestella who had nothing else to do with their strength. They wanted to test themselves, to fight with everything they had for once in their lives. And this was the only place in the world where they could unleash their powers with no reservations.

Ayato belonged to neither category.

"Yes, I'm fully aware that you have no interest whatsoever in those matters. I also know that you previously declined a scholarship offer." Claudia paused and swiveled her chair again to face Ayato. "However, our school's performance at the Festa in recent years has hardly been commendable. Last season, we finished in fifth place. Queenvale took last place, but considering that part of their strategy is to completely ignore their own rank, we might as well have finished last. We will do whatever it takes to break out of this sorry state of affairs, and to that end, we must acquire every promising student we can get our hands on."

The Festa was a broad term referring to a set of events—three categories, in fact, one taking place each year. The tag team doubles competition, Phoenix, took place in the summer of the first year; the team competition, Gryps, in the fall of the second year; and the individual competition, Lindvolus, in the winter of the third year. Points were awarded in each competition to the best performers and their schools, with the total results calculated at the end of the Lindvolus. A full "season" of the Festa was a three-year cycle.

And as Claudia had just mentioned, Seidoukan Academy's performance had been faltering for several seasons running.

"Students have the right to participate in the Festa three times. This is actually fairly limiting—even the most outstanding candidates can participate only three times. To be honest, I can't say that our school's roster is very deep."

Students were eligible to register for the Festa from ages thirteen to twenty-two—a span of a decade. With few exceptions, they were free to choose which Festa events they would participate in. For instance, some would fight in each competition of a single season and leave their schools in three years, whereas others would take nine years to compete only in the Lindvolus.

The more talented students a school had, the better. Which was why each school employed a number of keen-eyed scouts to gather fighters from across the globe. Tuition exemptions, living subsidies, equipment, and material support—while the specific amenities provided by each school varied, scholarship students were the ones specially singled out and invited.

"Why invite me on a special scholarship in the first place?" said

Ayato. "This is going to sound like I'm just being humble, but I really don't think I deserve that level of treatment."

"That's understandable. You were a complete unknown, and to tell the truth, our scouts raised some fierce objections when I put in your name."

"You mean—*you* nominated me?"

Students scouted out to be awarded scholarships were typically those who excelled in lower-level tournaments affiliated with the Festa or other competitions. Stregas and Dantes were exceptions, but compulsory national registration left them no escape from the scrutiny of scouts.

Ayato, meanwhile, was no more than the son of a swordsmanship dojo long in decline, and he had achieved nothing of significance in tournaments or anywhere else.

"Yes, and I pushed through your candidacy," she crowed. "I was never happier to be student council president. Three cheers for authority!"

"…That's pretty assertive."

"If you had turned us down, I would have completely lost face. I'm so glad you had a change of heart."

"Well, I didn't exactly have a change of heart…" As Ayato hunched his shoulders, Claudia narrowed her eyes.

"Then why come to this school?"

Ayato said nothing. And then suddenly, with a deadly serious look, he leaned in with both hands on the desk and stared straight into her eyes.

"Claudia, is it true that my sister was here? Haruka Amagiri—was she here?"

"Hmm, well. Regarding that…" Meeting his gaze unflinchingly, Claudia raised her index finger. "There's only one thing I know that might be relevant. Someone deleted the data on a *certain female student* who had once been enrolled in this school."

"Deleted it…? Is that even possible?"

"Under normal circumstances, no."

"Not even for a student council president?"

"The power of my office isn't absolute. But as for those above me…
Well." Claudia gave him a knowing smile.

Ayato's expression didn't break. By that, she could only mean the
integrated enterprise foundation.

"There's no record of that student ever participating in the Festa,
and she was never listed in the Named Chart. It's not clear whether
she ever attended this school at all. It was only five years ago—her
classmates and teachers would still be here. And yet not a single person remembers her. I'm not sure what can be done."

"What if the Festa records were altered, too?"

"Impossible. That would mean deceiving all of Asterisk itself,
along with the billions of Festa fans around the world. The Festa
is broadcast live worldwide; the Named Chart is publicly available
online and constantly updated. In this city, even spontaneous duels
get picked up by the media in the blink of an eye. Videos of your
duel with Julis are probably all over the Net already."

"But then—"

Cutting him off, Claudia entered something in the mobile device
by her hand. An air-window interface opened up in the space
between them, displaying an image of a single woman. Ayato's eyes
went wide.

"This is the only piece of data I was able to recover. She matriculated here five years ago, then left after half a year for personal reasons. Her name, her date of birth—there's basically nothing left of
any information that could identify her."

But this was more than enough for Ayato. It was her. There was no
mistake.

"How did you get this, Claudia?"

To recover data, one has to know that something was deleted to
begin with. But she had just told him that there was no record, nor
human memory, of this student's existence. So how did she know?

"I'm sorry, but I can't tell you that. Do you not believe me?"

"Oh— No, that's not what I mean," Ayato replied hurriedly. As student council president, she probably had her sources of information.

He was grateful to her for at least letting him know that she couldn't tell him.

"Now, this is my personal opinion, but…regardless of the particulars, I doubt she's still at this school. If she is the reason why you came here…" Claudia apologetically trailed off.

But Ayato regained his usual laid-back demeanor and shook his head. "No, it's okay. Thank you. But I didn't come here to look for my sister."

She looked at him inquisitively and repeated her earlier question. "Then why did you come to this school?"

"Umm…" He crossed his arms and gave it a few moments' thought, then answered with a short laugh, "If I have to have a reason… To find out what it is that I have to do, I guess?"

"Such a vague, formulaic answer."

"Huh, it is? I thought I'd managed to sound like a student."

Claudia laughed softly. "You're not so innocent yourself, are you?"

She seemed to think that he had dodged her question. But Ayato had meant to answer sincerely, in a sense. Maybe he really could find out here what he had to do. *If my sister was really here…*

"Oh, that's right!" she exclaimed with a clap of her hands. "I nearly forgot to tell you something important… The scholarship students at our school have several special privileges beyond exemptions in tuition and various fees. One of those is priority in the use of an Orga Lux."

"An Orga Lux? You mean the ones that use special manadite?"

"Yes, urm-manadite."

The meteorites that had fallen to Earth in the Invertia contained a previously unknown element known as mana and a particular ore known as manadite. Manadite was found to be composed of crystallized mana, and in recent years, methods had been developed to artificially manufacture it (although synthesized manadite was lower quality).

Research into mana and manadite had spearheaded a new field of science called "meteoric engineering," whose crowning achievement were the Luxes—mana-transforming weapons that used manadite in their cores. Once activated, they assembled the elemental blueprint embedded in the manadite's memory and generated blades (or projectiles) of concentrated mana.

Lux technology was superior in many respects to conventional weapons—power output could be adjusted at will, the activator fit in the palm of the hand, projectile-type Luxes required no stock of ammunition. With all the advantages in usability, most small-scale weapons produced today were Luxes. And Luxes had become so commonplace that low-power versions were sold for personal protection and as children's toys.

Rare manadite crystals of extraordinary purity were also found—urm-manadite. Orga Luxes used these crystals as their cores, producing output beyond comparison to normal Luxes. While they could bestow special abilities similar to those of Dantes and Stregas, they were also known for being difficult to wield.

The vast majority of Orga Luxes were controlled by the integrated enterprise foundations, but a few were entrusted to Asterisk schools for the purposes of data collection.

"There are people who don't care for Orga Luxes. Of course, you're not required to use one. And some of them can cause, well, side effects of a sort—we say they come with a 'cost.' What do you think?"

"Isn't there a compatibility rating or something?"

Whether or not an Orga Lux could be wielded to its full potential depended greatly on the user. Rumor held that an Orga Lux had a will of its own and would select its user accordingly.

"Yes—in fact, that is the most important factor. The standard here at Seidoukan Academy is eighty percent compatibility. Even if you find a weapon that you like, you will not be allowed to use it if your rating is any lower than that."

"I see..." Not that Ayato was completely uninterested, but going through all of that sounded like too much of a hassle. Anyway, he might not even meet the required compatibility rating.

As Ayato stood there thinking, he noticed the uncertain look on Claudia's face.

"Is something the matter?"

"Well, I wasn't sure I ought to tell you this, because I'm still trying to confirm it… But there's something suspicious about the Orga Lux lending records."

"What about them?"

"Naturally, the usage of any Orga Lux equipment is strictly supervised. The records of who took out which one and when are collected along with the battle data. But we identified one instance of an Orga Lux having battle data when there was no record of it being taken out for use."

"You mean…someone used it without permission?"

"Or they altered the lending records. That would be the more likely explanation. Those records are kept in the Matériel Department's computer bank, while the battle data is accumulated in each weapon's urm-manadite core. And there is still much we don't understand about the latter, so it might be that they tried to alter it and were unable to do so."

"Let me guess—the data is from five years ago."

"Precisely."

Ayato sighed heavily. "Then I'd really like to take a look."

At this point, he could infer the likelihood that his sister had once used the Orga Lux in question. Whether or not he would be permitted to use it, he at least wanted to see it with his own eyes.

"Very well. I'll contact you later with the details. In the meantime, please use this." Claudia held out a Lux activator. "It's an ordinary blade-type Lux. I've taken the liberty of calibrating it to your personal data, but please take it to the Matériel Department if you need any more adjustments made."

"Great, thank you. Wait, that reminds me…" Seeing the activator, Ayato remembered that he had been borrowing a Lux this whole time—the one that spectator had tossed to him before the duel with Julis. "This isn't good. How do I return it…?" He took it out and inspected it, but there was no name written on it.

She laughed gently. "Oh, it's quite all right. The school will supply any weapons and equipment a student might need."

"Really? That's…pretty generous." Luxes of a caliber to be used in actual combat were not cheap. Still, the cost was probably just a drop compared to the ocean of profits brought in by the Festa.

"Oh—I just remembered one more thing."

"Yes? What is it?"

"You were saying something earlier about the last technicalities to take care of for my transfer?"

"Oh yes. About that—" Claudia started, but her mouth closed mid-sentence. She seemed to be lost in thought and then looked all around her.

"…Something wrong?"

"Oh no! Not exactly…" She waved it off, but something clearly had her acting differently. Her cheeks were flushed as if with a fever, and she cast her gaze downward. "Um… Er, let's see— Would you mind closing your eyes for a moment?"

"Huh?" What kind of paperwork required him to close his eyes? That went through Ayato's mind, but he closed his eyes without thinking on it too much. He heard the chair squeak, then after a pause—

"Gotcha!"

A faint impact struck him in the back. He was a little surprised, but it didn't hurt. In fact, it felt soft. …*Too* soft.

"Wha—?" He had a guess as to what had happened. Opening his eyes tentatively, he saw two graceful arms wrapped around his midsection. He was being embraced from behind.

"Wh— Hey! C-Claudia!?"

Her only reply was a mischievous laugh.

Something with overwhelming mass and unparalleled softness was pressing against his back. If one were to describe it with onomatopoeia, *jiggle* or *squish* would certainly be appropriate choices.

Flustered, Ayato decided that he was being teased again. If that was the case, he should try to act undaunted and respond calmly. The operative word being *try*.

But there was a faint whisper from behind him…

"At last… We meet at last."

Her voice seemed so fragile, so helpless—the vulnerability of an irrepressible emotion. Against that candor, his cynicism dissipated like mist.

"Claudia...?" he said, but no answer came.

He wondered for a moment if they had met somewhere before, but he couldn't recall it. And there was no way he would forget such an exceptional girl. After they stood like that for a while—though it wasn't really that long—she smoothly released him.

"Ha-ha. Just kidding. Did I surprise you?"

Ayato turned to see her smiling as if nothing had happened at all. Caught off guard, he lost the chance to ask her what she'd meant. "Well...anyone would be surprised if someone hugged them from behind out of nowhere."

"Oh—please don't get me wrong. It's not as if I do things like this to everyone I meet. Actually, I'm very reserved." She put her hand to her mouth, and Ayato couldn't discern from her tone how serious she was.

"So, now what?"

"Yes?"

"That...couldn't have been the last technicality, right?" He changed the subject, trying to get back to the reason why she'd brought him here in the first place.

"Oh, that. That was a lie."

"...You lied?" Ayato's mouth hung open.

"A crime of expedience, you might say," Claudia said without a hint of shame. "You've officially been part of this institution for a while now. Not a single technicality left. That was simply the most effective way to bring that scene to a close. Julis is earnest if nothing else, so I knew that she wouldn't continue a duel in breach of the rules."

"Wait, but..."

"Would you rather I hadn't stopped her?"

"Um..." He had no response.

"How do you suppose things would have turned out if you two had continued? Neither the school nor I would want that."

Ayato could see what she meant by "blackhearted." He wasn't sure just how black her heart was, but the student council president who stood before him was much more than she seemed. The vulnerability she'd shown only seconds ago had already vanished without a trace.

"It's almost time for class now, so let's wrap this up, shall we? Please don't hesitate to get in touch if anything comes up. I'll do my best to be of help."

Even after all that, the smile on Claudia's face as she saw Ayato off was unquestionably beautiful.

*

"Yeah, so, this is the new scholarship student, Ayato Amagiri. Be nice, 'kay?"

Rather perfunctory as introductions went. A bit of consideration or empathy would have been nice, Ayato thought, for a transfer student worried about fitting in to his new class. He cast a sidelong glance at the woman standing next to him. But Kyouko Yatsuzaki, the homeroom teacher of Grade 10, Class 3, only jutted her chin at him slightly, as if to say, "*You're next.*"

She was slender and tall, with sharp eyes...*mean* eyes, actually, would be a more accurate description. Her manner of speech and demeanor were not teacherly at all, and to phrase it bluntly, she was somewhat vulgar.

What stuck out the most about her was an object she held: a baseball bat with nails driven into it. Ayato could see that it was well seasoned. It was an item that invited conflicting feelings—on one hand, he was very curious about the dark red stains on it, and on the other, he really didn't want to know at all.

"C'mon, I don't have all day," she pointed out.

"Oh yes, ma'am. Uh, I'm Ayato Amagiri. Hi."

Ayato managed no more than that brusque introduction himself, so maybe he wasn't one to judge.

His classmates regarded him with various expressions. Some

intrigued, some completely disinterested, others inspecting, and still others cautious…

One girl turned her gaze on Ayato with a very complicated look indeed, but he could understand that.

"So, your seat… Oh, there we go. There's an empty desk next to your friend who plays with fire. Take that one."

"Wh-who are you saying plays with fire!?" At Kyouko's words, the girl—that would be Julis—stood up with her face flushed bright red.

"Heh-heh. Who else would I be talking about, Riessfeld? Can't believe you put on a show like that first thing in the damn morning. If you were challenged, that'd be one thing—but it's kinda not the time for a Page One student to be starting fights willy-nilly. This isn't Le Wolfe, y'know."

With a small angry sound, Julis reluctantly took her seat in the second to last row. Beside her were two adjacent empty seats.

"Who knew we'd be in the same class?" Ayato remarked as he sat down next to her.

"If this is a joke, it's not funny." Julis ducked facedown on the desk and sighed heavily. Not the warmest of welcomes.

Undaunted, Ayato tried again. "We had an eventful morning, but…I hope we get along better."

Julis looked at him from the corner of her eye. "I owe you a debt. At your request, I'll do something to help you once. Other than that, you won't get the time of day from me." Then she turned decisively away from him.

…Okay, then.

"Oooh, rejected." From a seat behind him came a voice that was half-sympathetic and half-teasing.

Ayato turned to see a boy with a friendly smile on a strong-lined face, holding out his hand. "Well, it's the Princess, after all. What can you do?"

As Ayato offered his own hand, the other boy shook it gladly and vigorously.

"I'm Eishirou Yabuki. I'm your roommate, or so I'm told."

"Roommate? Oh, you mean in the dorm?"

"That's right. Most of our housing is double occupancy."

"So you had the room to yourself until now? Sorry to cut your space in half."

"Don't worry about it. The more the merrier, I say." Eishirou was one cheerful young man.

Ayato couldn't be sure when they were sitting down, but Eishirou seemed to be a full head taller than him. He carried himself like a boy, but his build and expressions seemed very much grown-up. The rather conspicuous scar on his left cheek only added to his contradictory charm.

"Anyway, if I'm going to be sharing my room, I was hoping it'd be with somebody interesting."

"…Um, I'm not that interesting, though."

"Oh, come on. You dueled a Page One the morning of your first day, and *then* you jumped the Princess in front of a whole crowd. No need to be so modest."

For his part, Ayato didn't have an iota of intent to be modest. He could have spent an hour explaining himself with regards to those events, but it would appear that rumor had beaten him to it, and a certain impression of him had already infiltrated the student body.

And indeed, no sooner was homeroom over than a small crowd formed around Ayato.

"Hey, Amagiri, isn't it a weird time of year to transfer? What'd you do at the school you were at before?"

"So why were you dueling the Princess in the first place? I can't find any intel about that at all!"

"No, no, no—we want to hear about the romance! That intense overture! C'mon, tell us! Did you fall for her in the middle of a duel? The pangs of forbidden love?"

"Hold on! Forget that garbage—tell us how to beat the Princess! How were you dodging those attacks?"

"He's right. To be honest, I never thought you'd last that long."

On the other hand, some were much more callous.

"Hah. Isn't it obvious? The Glühen Rose was holding back!"

"True, true. His movements, his reaction time—totally mediocre by this city's standards. At that rate, he'll never make the Named Chart."

"How is he a scholarship student? Do our scouts need their eyes checked?"

On and on.

This repeated at the end of every class period, so that by the time school was out for the day, Ayato was completely drained.

"Whew..."

The late afternoon sun poured into the classroom where he was flopped listlessly in his seat.

Eishirou tapped him on the shoulder. "Long day, huh? Must be hard being that popular."

"Well, I was able to pick up some things, though."

"Oh? Like what?"

"For starters, I'm not the popular one—it's Julis." Ayato glanced at the desk next to his and shrugged his shoulders theatrically. The inhabitant of that desk was long gone, having left the moment class ended. "None of them are interested in me. They just want to hear about the guy who dueled Julis. Right?"

"Ooh, very perceptive!" Eishirou applauded, giving him a most approving look.

"But then, wouldn't it be easier if they just asked Julis herself?"

"Yeah, easier said than done. She's not exactly easy to talk to, you know?"

"Now that you mention it, she doesn't seem very approachable."

Still, remembering her smile as she clutched that handkerchief to her, Ayato couldn't imagine that she was the type to spurn any and all human contact.

"Well, I don't know why," said Eishirou, "but the Princess keeps people at more than arm's length, that's for sure. Besides—"

"Oh, wait. I feel dumb asking this now, but is 'Princess' her nickname or something? Everyone seems to call her that."

"Um, well, sort of, but...she's also a real, live, literal princess."

"Huh?" Ayato couldn't believe what he'd just heard. "A princess... like, a fairy-tale princess?"

"Yup. The kind that gets cursed by an evil witch and awakened by a kiss from a prince, gets offered in marriage for political purposes, comes from a magical kingdom, gets attacked by orcs and tentacles. A princess."

Ayato thought something was a little off about the last part there, but he could understand what Eishirou meant to say.

"You know how after the Invertia, places all across Europe started reverting to monarchies? Well, I guess for an integrated enterprise foundation, it must've been convenient to have figurehead royalty around while they took political and economic control. Anyway, she's the first crown princess of a country called Lieseltania. Her full name is Julis-Alexia Marie Florentia Renate von Riessfeld. That's in the registry of European royal families."

"Wow... You sure know a lot about her."

"Well, it's my business. I'm in the newspaper club." Eishirou grinned triumphantly.

"But why is a princess fighting in a place like this? Don't princesses usually sit around being graceful?" Ayato wondered, recalling how he was nearly burned to a crisp that morning. True, she had elegance, dignity, and style all in spades, but her will to fight seemed just a bit excessive.

"Now that, I don't know. I'd love to ask her myself, actually." Eishirou nodded in earnest and added to himself, "That'd be front-page material for sure..."

Then he went on, "Of course, seeing as she's that pretty, and strong, and a princess to boot—no one would leave her alone. She came to this school last year, and if you think what you got today was bad, that was nothing compared to the Princess Fever. Before you could blink, she had a crowd of people around her, bombarding her with questions."

"I can picture it."

"And then, what do you think she told 'em? 'Pipe down! Shut up! I am not a spectacle to be gawked at!'"

"I can picture that, too."

"Well, most people backed off after that, but there were some who didn't like her attitude. So a bunch of them challenged her to one duel after another—and she took them all down. Before anyone knew what was happening, boom, she was a Page One."

That only seemed natural. Ayato knew, from having faced her in battle, that Julis possessed considerable skill. He couldn't imagine there were many students stronger than her, not even here in Asterisk.

"And there you have it. A princess holding herself so aloof that everyone backs away from her. There aren't many around now with the guts to face her head-on and speak to her."

"Huh... But then, does she have any friends?"

"Not a single one. That I know of, anyway... Sorry. Hold on a sec." Eishirou held up one hand to pause the conversation and pulled the lightly vibrating mobile device from his pocket. "Hey, what's up, chief?"

An air-window popped open to show a woman in a short bob who immediately launched into a diatribe. *"Don't you 'hey-what's-up' me! I told you I needed that proof from you first thing this morning! What the hell are you doing?"*

"Oh, my bad! Something else came up this morning—"

"I don't need your excuses! Get your butt over here! In five minutes or else!" The window closed with a blip.

Eishirou smiled sheepishly and scratched his nose. "Well, you heard that. I better get going."

"Okay. I should head to the dorm, anyway."

"Right. See you back there."

"Oh, wait... Yabuki!" Just as Eishirou was leaving the classroom, Ayato tossed him the object he'd been holding.

"Huh?" Surprised, Eishirou caught it, then smirked as he saw what it was. "Oh. So you figured it out, huh?"

"I guess I should thank you. Although I'm not totally sure about that, since Julis might have let me go if not for that thing." It was a Lux activator—not the one Claudia had given him, but the one Ayato had borrowed earlier that morning.

"How'd you know it was me?"

"Hmm. Your voice, I guess," Ayato replied breezily.

Eishirou stared at him blankly for a moment.

"You're telling me that you remembered my voice, one guy out of a crowd, in a situation like that?"

"My big sister always told me to return anything I borrow."

"*Ha-ha!* You are pretty interesting, after all." Eishirou made his shoulders shake with laughter, trying to disguise the fact that his cheeks were burning. "Hey, Amagiri. You really think you couldn't have won that duel?"

"No. Not at where I am now." That was the plain truth.

"Hmm. Where you are now, huh?" Perhaps satisfied with that response, Eishirou strode lightly out of the classroom.

Ayato stared at the door after him for a bit, then let out a deep sigh. "This school's gonna be a lot tougher than I thought…"

CHAPTER 3
HER NOBLE EYES

"Huh? Oh, come on. I can't go this way?"

Ayato had tried to cut through the courtyard, thinking it would be a shortcut to the dorms, but found himself stuck at a metal barrier.

Apparently, the school closed some of the gates in the evening.

The gate wasn't all that high, and Ayato could have gone over it—but that was exactly what had landed him in so much trouble this morning. Better to just head back and find another way.

"Oh, well… It's not like I'm in a hurry." Taking walks, after all, was one of the few things Ayato liked to do for fun.

The courtyard was as spacious as an average-sized park, with impeccably maintained greenery. Looking around, Ayato saw several humanoid robots that resembled featureless dolls—Puppets—pruning the trees. While he had heard somewhere that Puppets for military use could be remote-controlled, the ones in common use were entirely automated, slow-moving and able to handle only simple tasks. By now, Puppets like these had largely taken over the realm of harsh physical labor.

Still, this was not a sight commonly seen in provincial towns like the one Ayato had come from.

He was walking between the sharp silhouettes of trees against the setting sun, curiously watching the Puppets at work, when an angry shout suddenly echoed through the courtyard: "Then why the hell did you duel that new kid!?"

It was a young male voice, ferocious enough to freeze a faint-hearted listener in his tracks, making the air crackle with tension.

Some kind of argument...? thought Ayato.

Keeping himself hidden in the shadows, he peered through the trees to find a small gazebo in a clearing. In front of it were three male students. The boy in the middle stood out, tall and sturdy with a muscular build, intimidating even from a distance. The other two—one thin and one fat—stood a step behind, giving the sense that they deferred to the tall boy.

They seemed to be talking to someone inside the gazebo, but from his vantage point, Ayato couldn't see who it was.

If someone was in trouble, he could hardly just walk away—but at the same time, he would rather not poke his nose in where he wasn't wanted. All the more so considering that this school had its own set of rules, to which Ayato was only just starting to acclimate.

Still...

"Tell me, Julis!"

Hearing that name, Ayato automatically leaned closer.

"I don't have to tell you anything, Lester. We all have the right to duel whomever we please."

"You're right. That goes for me, too."

Ayato moved sneakily from tree to tree, and there she was—a girl with shining rose-red hair sitting in the gazebo. She and the student named Lester glared at one another so fiercely one could practically see sparks flying. The situation hardly seemed amicable.

"We also have the right to refuse," said Julis. "You can challenge me all you want, but I have no intention of dueling you again."

"Then tell me why!"

"You really need it spelled out for you?" Julis sighed heavily and stood up to face Lester. "It's because this will never end. I've bested you three times. There's no point in us fighting again."

"I'll beat you this time! Don't let that string of lucky breaks go to your head! You haven't seen my *real* power!"

"That's right! You wouldn't stand a chance if Lester went all out!" One of the pair standing behind Lester, the fat one tried to score points by jeering at Julis.

"Then prove it to someone else." Julis turned away, declaring an end to their conversation.

"Hey! This isn't over—!"

Just as Lester reached out to grab her shoulder, Ayato stepped out from behind the trees and blurted, "Oh, it's you, Julis! What a coincidence, running into you in a place like this."

"…What are *you* doing here?"

"Who the hell're you?"

Ayato's timing and words made for such a transparent act that both Julis and Lester looked daggers at him.

He forced an awkward laugh and fumbled, "Well, um, I got a little lost…"

"Oh, hey! Lester! That's him—the new kid!"

"What…!?" Lester impaled Ayato with an even sharper glare. If a gaze had physical force, Lester's would have blasted through a sheet of metal.

But Ayato calmly let it roll over him. "So, Julis, who's this?" he asked.

Julis answered him with her hand on her hip, looking at him as if he were something ridiculous. "Lester MacPhail. He's ranked ninth."

"Huh, so you're a Page One, too," Ayato remarked, turning to Lester. "Wow!"

Lester said nothing.

"Oh yeah—I'm Ayato Amagiri. Nice to meet you."

Lester kept staring balefully down at him, without so much as a glance at Ayato's extended right hand.

Up close, Lester's size was even more impressive. He had to be almost seven feet tall, with broad shoulders and bulging, honed muscles.

Genestella musculature was far more powerful and limber than that of ordinary humans, but it was largely resistant to bodybuilding efforts. Which meant Lester must have worked unbelievably hard to achieve his current physique.

He had short, bristling brown hair over a chiseled face that was currently full of fury.

"You…you fought a little brat like this, but you won't fight me…?" Lester growled, his clenched fists trembling. "The hell with that! I'm going to crush you! No matter what it takes!"

Apparently Ayato didn't even register to him. Lester stepped up toward Julis with a belligerent swagger.

"H-hey, Lester, take it easy! This can't be the best place…" The thin boy tried to calm him down, but Lester didn't seem to hear.

Julis was around average height for a girl her age, so that next to Lester she looked like a child beside an adult, but she stood there undaunted. "That's unlikely. Unless you do something about that charging-boar personality of yours, I will beat you every time."

"Wha—? Damn it!" Lester was on the verge of exploding in rage, but realized that doing so would only lend more truth to her words.

"Y-you better take Lester seriously, or you're gonna regret it! He'll get you next time, just wait and—"

"Enough, Randy!" Lester barked at the pudgy boy and stepped down from the gazebo with a sour sneer. "I'm not giving up," he spat. "Not until I make you see my true strength…!"

He left Julis with that and the two sidekicks hurried after him.

"What a bother," she sighed once the boys were completely out of sight and took a seat again on the bench.

Ayato laughed under his breath. "Maybe I shouldn't have done anything?"

"I'll say. Thanks to you, he was even more annoying than usual."

"Sorry… Wait, that's *usual*, though?"

Julis shrugged in reply. "Apparently, he doesn't care for me. He's not alone in that, but he's the first one to be so persistent about it."

"But he's ranked ninth, so he must be pretty strong, right?" Ayato was about to ask if she would be okay but caught himself. Even one day's acquaintance was enough for him to understand that taking that sort of tone with her would set off her temper.

"If we're talking about fighting ability, yes, he's strong. But not as strong as me, and rankings aren't all that reliable to begin with. There are plenty of skilled fighters who aren't in the Named Chart. There's also the matter of chemistry—how you match up against a particular opponent."

Julis lifted her gaze to him, the corners of her mouth curling up slightly, as if she expected something. Ayato averted his eyes.

"Since we're here, I have a question of my own," she said.

"Um…wh-what do you want to know?"

"You used Meteor Arts in our duel this morning. How did you do it with an uncalibrated Lux?"

"Oh, that wasn't Meteor Arts."

"You're serious?"

"I can't use Meteor Arts in the first place. I don't think I get along with Luxes—well, it's just not for me. I'd rather have a real physical weapon."

"Then, that technique from this morning…"

"That was just a sword technique. My family has a traditional swordsmanship dojo going way back, so I know a few."

"*Just* a sword technique?" Julis's eyes widened. "Granted, it's not impossible to cut through my flames with a Lux blade. But I've never seen anyone slice them in half as cleanly as you did. Exactly how good are you?"

"Oh, I was just lucky," Ayato laughed.

"…Hmph. Fine. We'll see how long you can keep up that innocent act. This place isn't as nice as you think."

"I don't really think that at all…" Ayato scratched the back of his head. "What about you, Julis? Why are you fighting in such a dangerous place?"

"What?"

"I heard…you're a princess."

"It's true—I am the first crown princess of Lieseltania. And so what? Everyone here, to some extent, is fighting for something that they can't obtain anywhere else. Titles and status have nothing to do with it." She spoke quietly, but her words held a fierce, unwavering resolve.

He hesitated, wondering if he would be going too far, but then he posed the question anyway. "...So what do you want?"

Julis gave him an unexpectedly straight answer. "Money."

"Huh...?"

"I need money. And fighting here is the fastest way to get it."

A princess, fighting for money? He would have thought that a princess would be plenty wealthy. Then why...?

"I need it quickly," she went on. "And the timing is convenient. I'll go undefeated in all of this season's Festas. That's my objective."

"All three Festas...?"

The so-called "grand slam." Even Ayato knew how difficult that was.

"Yes, and I'll start with the Phoenix," said Julis. "I have to win that, at the very least."

The amount of Festa prize money was determined based on the points earned, but winning even one event, Ayato had heard, would gain you enough to spend the rest of your life in leisure.

He wanted to ask why but decided against it. He had that much discretion. But what little he'd heard answered a different question for him.

"Oh, so that's why you're looking for a partner?" said Ayato, recalling the exchange that morning between Claudia and Julis.

The Phoenix was a tag team tournament, so of course Julis could not participate on her own.

She flinched a bit. "...W-well, yes."

Her reticence on the subject seemed to indicate that she really was having some difficulty finding a partner. Maybe that was inevitable, given her personality...

"I—I may not have found a partner yet—but that's not because I don't have any friends! I mean, it's true that I don't have friends at this school, but that isn't the issue. There simply isn't anyone who meets my standards as a partner."

So she admits that she doesn't have any friends? Ayato thought but stayed away from that. "Then what kind of partner are you looking for?"

"Well… First of all, someone as good as me—but I know that's asking for too much. So someone with at least the abilities of a Page One, a person of impeccable integrity, who thinks well on their feet, with a strong will and a noble spirit. Someone with the qualities of a knight."

"…You're setting the bar pretty high," Ayato remarked.

"Hmm, really? I thought I was being fairly lenient…"

Maybe that was the princess in her talking.

"Although the entry deadline *is* getting close, I suppose I can't be too picky at this point," Julis said under her breath, as if talking to herself, then picked up her bag and stood. "It's about time I was leaving… But what were you doing here, anyway?"

"Oh, well, um… I thought it'd be quicker to go this way, but the gate over there was locked."

"It would be. The courtyard gates close automatically at night. At this hour, though, the only ones that are shut should be on the middle school side."

So I was completely *lost*, Ayato thought with chagrin.

"Wait, so if the gates close automatically, does that mean that I'll be trapped if I hang out in here too long?" he wondered. "Should I be worried about that?"

"Huh?"

"I mean, um, I like to walk around places like this, but I wouldn't want to get stuck…"

Julis stared at him blankly for a moment, then burst into laughter.

"Well, obviously! Are you really that dumb? After the mess you got yourself into this morning, you didn't even bother to look at a campus map!? Don't worry—the high school gates stay open until the middle of the night," she said teasingly, and her eyes narrowed with a smile. She looked right then like a normal girl…

"Hmm? What?" she said, noticing his silence.

"Oh… I was just thinking, so you *do* laugh."

"Wh…!?" The color rose to her face before his eyes. "Wh-what are you talking about!? I laugh sometimes, just like anybody else!"

Then her expression regained its usual sullen cast, and she turned away in a huff.

"Then why don't you act more friendly to start with?" said Ayato. "You could if you wanted to…"

"Shut up! That's none of your business!" Julis snapped. "Wh-who are you to talk, anyway? Why don't you get that spaced-out face of yours in order? A slack face reveals a careless mind! If you carried yourself better, maybe you wouldn't be making such stupid blunders, like you have all day today!"

That seems like a stretch, he thought, but conceded. "Well, okay—I was being careless, but also, I just don't know enough about this place…"

This campus was too big, to start with. And there were so many strange rules. Not at all easy for a newcomer. Maybe if there had been someone to show him around…

"Oh!" With that thought, Ayato looked straight at her.

"Wh-what now…?" For some reason, she blushed and took a step backward.

"Julis, would you show me around the school? Oh, and maybe the city, too, while we're on the subject."

"…Huh?" Julis didn't bother to hide her displeasure at the request. "Is that a joke? Why would I do that?"

"Well, you owe me a 'debt,' right? You said so yourself—I can ask you one favor."

"I did say that, but… Are you serious?"

"Serious…?"

"I mean, is *that* enough to repay the debt I owe you? I don't like it one bit, but you did save me this morning. That's no small debt. You could have anything you want from me, within reason— Th-that is, nothing indecent, of course! But for instance, I could lend you my strength as a Page One."

"You mean, you'd help me out in a fight?"

"Yes."

"No, that's okay." Ayato shook his head. "I think I'd better get used to this school first."

At this nonchalant reply, Julis gave him a searching stare, then smiled sarcastically and sighed. "You're a man of mysterious depths. Or maybe you really are an idiot?"

"If those are the two possibilities…I'm probably the latter," Ayato admitted.

"Hmph. Probably. But very well. I'll show you around, if that's what you want."

"Thanks. I appreciate it!"

"W-well, I don't have much choice, do I? A debt is a debt. I'll show you around campus after school tomorrow. As for the city…well, I'll have to set aside one of my days off for you."

"Great. I'm looking forward to it." *That should solve some of my most immediate problems*, he thought. "Okay, I guess I better find my own dorm now… *Ghk!*"

As Ayato started to walk away, Julis grabbed his collar from behind.

"Let me give you one tip right now. The fastest way to the boys' dorm from here is to go by the college building."

Choking, he managed to answer, "Th-thanks for that. But I'd appreciate it if maybe you could be a little more gentle with your lessons…"

As Ayato wheezed against the pressure around his throat, Julis replied with a faint smile, "Too bad. You failed to specify that in the terms of our agreement."

*

It was completely dark by the time Ayato arrived at the boys' dorm, which was situated on the opposite side of the school buildings from the girls' dorm. The girls' building sported a classical European facade, but this one looked like a conventional apartment high-rise.

"Let's see, room 211…" This time, Ayato made sure to check on the map before heading to the room.

While they were split into separate wings, middle school and college students shared the same floors as the high school students. Ayato found that somewhat refreshing. Every student who saw him walking by gave him a curious stare, which was bewildering, but he decided not to let it bother him and returned the attention with smiles and waves.

Room 211 was a corner room on the second floor. A fresh nameplate bore the name AYATO AMAGIRI. He knocked cautiously before entering.

"Hey, there you are. Took you long enough." Eishirou, lying on his bed, waved lazily in greeting.

"Yeah, it was one thing after another... Wow, this is bigger than I thought." His room was about two hundred square feet and came with a bed and desk. A single bag, casually placed atop the brand-new sheets, contained the few belongings that Ayato had arranged to have shipped.

"Is that all your stuff? You didn't bring much."

"Yeah, just enough to wear. You don't seem to have a lot either, though."

There were some handwritten notes and piles of papers on Eishirou's desk, but other than that, it was practically bare.

"I don't have a lot of hobbies. Just my work with the newspaper."

"Oh, that reminds me," said Ayato. "I've got a question for you, Mr. Reporter. There's this student called Lester—what kind of a guy is he?"

"Lester? Lester MacPhail?"

"That sounds right... Someone was saying he's ranked ninth."

"That'd be him. Lester, the Ax of the Roaring Distance." Eishirou sat up and touched his mobile to call up an air-window. It showed the very same tall, sturdy male student whom Ayato had met earlier.

"Lester MacPhail. First-year at Seidoukan Academy High School, Page One, ninth place. He excels at physical combat that allows him to make use of his body, and he's peerless in close combat. But he tends to struggle against opponents with special powers like Stregas and Dantes. He wields an ax-shaped Lux, the Bardiche-Leo."

"Wow, you're good!"

"Well, that was all information you can find on the Net. If you want something more, that's a different story."

"What do you mean?"

"I mean this." Eishirou meaningfully rubbed his thumb and fingers together.

"You're going to charge me!?"

"Come on, what did you expect? The students at this school—actually, the others are pretty much the same, too, so the students of Asterisk—mostly fall into two categories. One is those who are going all out to fight in the Festa, like the Princess. And the other is people who've long since given up on the Festa—like me."

"Yabuki, you're not even going to try?"

"Nope. It's not like just any Genestella can win here. If you've been here awhile, you can't help but notice the differences in people's strength. And you realize there are barriers you can't overcome. So, the question is, what do people who've dropped out of the competition do?"

"What do they *do*? I don't know."

As Ayato began to get lost in thought, Eishirou laughed and puffed out his chest. "Simple! We find things we want to do and ways to make money that aren't fighting in the Festa. For me, it's the school newspaper."

"I had no idea being in the newspaper club was so lucrative." Making money for personal gain was not an activity that one usually associated with student clubs.

"Hey, have some respect. Not to toot my own horn, but we do pretty well, y'know. You must've seen images of Asterisk on the Net or on TV. If it's a picture taken on a campus, you can bet it came from one of the student journalism clubs. There's a convention against outside media setting foot on campus."

Now it made sense. "Ha-ha, I get it... So you and your fellow reporters sell those kinds of images and information to media companies."

"Bingo!" Eishirou grinned and raised a finger. "There are lots of others who run a trade. Like the Society for the Study of Meteoric Engineering... They take on work customizing Luxes, and they're way better at it than the Matériel Department. Well, no match for Allekant—they're the best at technology out of the six schools—but still. And don't go saying this too loud, but a lot of the gambling around school duels has students as the bookies."

"The school doesn't crack down on that kind of thing?" It seemed to Ayato that gambling and bookmaking strayed far outside the realm of student activities.

But Eishirou wagged his uplifted finger and clicked his tongue. "Who's going to raise an objection these days to money changing hands? The IEFs run all the schools in the first place."

The integrated enterprise foundations prioritized the stimulation and development of economic activity. Essential to that objective was the flow of cash, and consumerism was encouraged as a global trend. Asterisk, too, was built with all that firmly in mind.

"And what else…?" Eishirou went on. "Right, there are some that join the entourage of stronger students. Especially Page One students. There are a lot of perks to being close to them."

"Oh? Is that… Does Lester have people like that?" Ayato remembered the two students standing behind Lester.

"You mean these guys?" Eishirou opened two more air-windows, one displaying the thin boy and the other one the pudgy boy. While their physical features made for a sharp contrast, they had the same obsequious look in their eyes.

"Yeah, it's them."

"The skinny one is Silas Norman. He is a Dante, but doesn't have much to show for it. Some telekinetic powers. The fat one is Randy Hooke. He was in the Named Chart once, but not anymore. He uses a bow Lux."

"You really are good with intel…" Ayato was honestly dumbfounded. It was one thing to keep track of the strongest students—but having ready knowledge of their hangers-on to boot was on another level.

"Heh. Impressed you, did I?" Laughing, Eishirou closed the air-windows and leaped off the bed. "Okay, then. Let's get something to eat. I'll show you the cafeteria."

"Before we go, there's one more thing I want to ask about Lester."

"Oh?"

"Is there...something between him and Julis?"

Eishirou grinned at the question. "Oh, *I* get it. I was wondering why you wanted to know so much about this guy all of a sudden. You really are after the Princess, huh?"

"Th-that's not it, at all..." It was true, though, that the girl was on his mind a lot, for reasons Ayato couldn't explain.

"It's fine, I don't care. But like I said before, it'll cost you."

Eishirou waited for Ayato to nod in consent, then opened another air-window.

This one showed a video. A girl wielding swaths of flame danced brilliantly on the display. Opposing her was a giant of a boy. He was swinging around an ax the size of his huge body, but it was clear that he was losing the fight.

"This is from last year's official ranking matches. Lester was ranked fifth at the time. The Princess was seventeenth."

"You mean..."

"Yup. She won. This is the fight that made her Page One. A match to remember."

"And for Lester, a match he'd rather forget."

"You could say that. In fact, Lester challenged the Princess in two more official matches, and he lost spectacularly."

Official matches were selective examinations held once a month by the school. Because the consent of both parties was necessary to duel, one could decline indefinitely. To prevent high-ranking students from using that as a loophole to keep their position, they were required to fight at least once a month. As a rule, in an official match, a high-ranking student did not have the right to decline a challenge from a lower-ranked student.

"Still, you can only challenge the same student twice," Eishirou explained. "Otherwise, you might have people throwing matches."

"So that means Lester can't challenge Julis again in an official match." *That's why he's so obsessed with dueling her,* Ayato thought.

"Lester has a lot of pride and a temper to go with it. It's probably driving him crazy, not getting back at her. I don't think he stands a chance, though," said Eishirou, pocketing his mobile. "What do you think?"

In that matchup, Lester was at a disadvantage, but he did have considerable skill. Luck counted for something in a fight, too, so nothing was certain.

"Going from that video, I don't think it's impossible for him," said Ayato. "But...their eyes are different."

"Hmm," Eishirou mused.

Julis's eyes weren't seeing Lester in that video—they were fixed on something far away, beyond her opponent. In contrast, Lester's eyes were focused on Julis alone. At that rate, Lester couldn't hold a candle to Julis.

But her far-off gaze... Ayato had seen something like it before.

"Thanks, Yabuki. So, what's that intel come to?" As a scholarship student, Ayato wasn't charged tuition or matriculation fees. But he didn't exactly have a lot of money. In fact, his family's run-down dojo was on the verge of shutting its doors. He did have some spending money saved up from part-time jobs, but if he wasn't frugal with it, he might run out quickly.

"All right! Time to eat! Let's get going, Amagiri!" Eishirou forcefully draped his arm around Ayato's neck and more or less dragged him out of the room. "We get a choice between the Japanese meal and the western meal. What'll it be?"

"Uh, um, then Japanese, I guess...?"

"The Japanese option today is grilled marinated Spanish mackerel, fried tofu, and stew of daikon radish and fish paste... Okay, I'll take your fried tofu."

"...Huh?"

"That's my fee this time. Consider it a new student discount." Eishirou grinned, then unwrapped his arm from Ayato's neck and clapped him on the back. "See? Aren't I a great guy?"

"I might think so...if you didn't say so about yourself." Ayato smiled and returned a slap to his roommate's back.

CHAPTER 4
REMINISCENCE AND REUNION

It was an early summer night with the scent of fresh grass rising in the air.

That day, the boy had been made to kneel in *seiza*, the traditional Japanese manner, back held rigid and behind resting on his heels, in a corner of the dojo. The pain showed on his childishly charming face only as a sulk, faintly illuminated in the gloom. He didn't even know anymore how long he had been in that position. Still, he refused to move from it, out of his own pride and defiance.

Suddenly, a door opened and a gentle voice wafted in, accompanied by the moonlight. "Honestly... What did you do this time? Dad was furious."

"I didn't do anything wrong," said the boy, pouting, and turned away.

The girl who had opened the door crouched down with her back to the moonlight and let out a curt sigh.

She pushed back her long black hair and looked down at the boy with a troubled gaze. She was five or six years older than him, brimming with energy that was complemented by her short-sleeved sailor suit uniform.

"Ayato."

"But, sis! Those guys—"

"Ayato!" The edge in her voice made the boy flinch. "A real man doesn't make excuses."

He had been holding back by sheer force of will, until now. His face twisted and his eyes filled with tears.

"But if you're really sorry, then I'll listen to your side of the story," she said.

"Really?" Now his expression lit up brightly.

"Are you sorry?"

"Yes, I'm sorry!"

"You won't do it again?"

"Nope!"

"Really and truly?"

"Uh-huh!"

"Really, really truly?"

"Hey, sis, remember when Saya was saying that no one likes girls who take things too seriously?"

Bonk. The girl's fist came down on his head.

"I'm sorry. I mean it."

"Very well." She nodded gravely. "Sit there."

"But I'm already sitting."

"S-sit down properly! *Seiza!*"

"I've *been* sitting in *seiza.*"

The girl cleared her throat, face reddening, and took a pair of glasses from the pocket of her uniform.

"I always wonder if you'd be better off just wearing your glasses all the time, instead of trying to look cool," said the boy.

"You shut up! I'll do what I want with my glasses!" The conservative black-framed glasses suited her face nicely, but she didn't care for them. "So. What happened?"

Finally, he thought, they were getting to the point. The story tumbled out of him. "I didn't do anything! They just kept bothering me for a match and wouldn't let up!"

According to the boy, the altercation began when some students at the dojo teased him for doing nothing but swinging his sword at practice.

His father strictly forbade him from sparring or fighting with the other students. Sometimes they picked on him for it.

The dojo didn't have many students, but most of them were Genestella, since the government had recommended martial arts as a way for Genestella to train their minds and build character.

The boy had his doubts about that. The others just wanted to show off their own strength.

There were harsh laws in place to punish any acts of violence by Genestella against civilians. And minors received no leniency, which might have been why Ayato, as a fellow Genestella boy, found himself a target of teasing.

"*And* they said bad things about you…!" The boy angrily chewed his lip.

The girl was also among those studying swordsmanship at the dojo. While she was not forbidden as strictly as her brother from engaging in combat, she almost never faced the other students. The students in question here had only joined the dojo recently, and they had never seen her in a match.

But the boy knew that his sister was the most skilled student at the dojo.

"That's why I agreed to fight them!" the boy blustered. "Just for a little bit—!"

The girl didn't need to hear the results to know what they were.

"Hmm." She thought quietly for a few moments and chose her words carefully when she spoke. "I see. I agree that you're not at fault, Ayato."

"I told you!" The boy looked up at her happily.

She pinned him with a stare and added reprovingly, "At the same time, you're not in the right, either."

"Huh?"

"Ayato, do you know why Dad forbids you from fighting anyone?"

The boy shook his head. He had asked his father the very same question himself but never received an answer.

"You have great strength inside you. But sometimes, strength can hurt people. And you could even hurt yourself, Ayato."

"But I'm not hurt at all, see? I don't hurt anywhere..."

"That's because you're still relying on your strength." The girl's voice went a little harder. "As long as you're giving yourself up to your own strength that way, you won't feel pain. But at the same time, you won't be able to feel the pain of others, either. Dad and I don't want you to grow up to be that kind of person, Ayato."

He looked at her blankly.

"Everyone has the right to fight for their dignity. That's why you're not at fault. But you don't know how to take responsibility for your actions yet. And you can never be right if you're not responsible."

"...I don't get it." He knew that she was telling him something important, but he could hardly understand any of it.

"It means you're not ready yet."

"Then when will I be ready?"

"Hmm, I don't know." Thinking, the girl touched her chin and tilted her head. "If I had to say... Maybe when you find out what it is that you have to do, Ayato."

"What I have to do...?"

"Yes. That'll come when you've decided how to use the strength you have."

The things she was saying were still a little too complicated for him, but the boy gave a small nod.

"Very good." Satisfied, the girl nodded, too, and patted her brother's head.

Something occurred to him, then. "What about you, sis?" he asked.

"Hmm?"

"Have you found the thing you have to do?"

For a moment, she looked surprised by the question but then gently smiled at him. "Of course. The thing I have to do...," the girl began and leaned down to hug her brother tight. "...Is protect you, Ayato."

"Me...?"

"That's right. It's the most important thing in the world to me."

"Then I'm going to protect you, too, sis! That's the thing I have to do!" The boy was completely serious. To him, too, it really did seem like the most precious and important thing there was.

But the girl smiled mischievously, then flicked his forehead with her finger and laughed. "What a thing to say! Don't you know you have to be stronger than me to say that?"

For that, he had no retort. He knew that his sister was far stronger than him.

"Besides, you have to be careful with promises like that. You're a boy, so a day will come when someone really wants to hear it from you."

"I don't get it." The boy hung his head, dejected.

She squeezed him again, much more tightly than before. "I know. That's okay for now."

"...Sis?"

"Thanks for sticking up for me, Ayato. I love you."

*

Tossing aside the light blanket, he sprang up out of bed like a jack-in-the-box.

He glanced at the clock to see that it was a little after four in the morning. Outside the window there was nothing but predawn shadows.

"There I go dreaming about memories again..."

Ayato managed to turn off the alarm almost as soon as it started beeping and then began to do his stretches. Habit was a fearsome power. After *that* day, he had been completely exhausted, but he now found himself wide awake at his usual hour.

"The timing saved me today, though," he said to himself. If he'd dreamed the rest...

Ayato shook his head forcefully and began to get dressed in his workout shirt and shorts rather than his uniform.

He thought about how this morning regimen was another thing

that his sister taught him. How many things had she given him—in the place of the mother he'd lost at such a young age, and as herself, his strict but kindhearted sister?

"Oh, so that's who she reminded me of...," Ayato realized. Julis's gaze in that video of the fight was the same as his sister's. Her eyes when she said she would protect him. They were the eyes of someone with an unbreakable resolve—eyes that he just didn't have yet.

"Okay..." He took the Lux activator from where he'd left it by his pillow and put it in the holster at his hip. Now he was ready. He would have rather had the wooden practice sword he'd been using at home, but he'd decided it was too bulky to bring.

As he tried to sneak out without waking his roommate, a cheery voice piped up from behind him. "Heading out for your morning training, Mr. Scholarship Student? What a conscientious pupil!"

He turned to see Eishirou still lying in bed with one eye open, showing his white teeth in a grin.

"Sorry, I didn't mean to wake you."

"Don't worry about it. I'm a light sleeper. Still half-asleep, actually." Scratching his head, Eishirou swallowed a yawn. "Well, I thought I heard someone talking in his sleep, but it must've been a dream."

The color drained from Ayato's face.

"Uh, Yabuki? I'm sure that you dreamed it. Totally sure. But just out of curiosity—could you tell me what the person in your dream was saying in their sleep?"

"'I really love you, too, sis!'"

Ayato shouted in protest and dashed over to clap his hands over his roommate's mouth. "Yes, that was a dream! Definitely a dream!" he repeated, trying desperately to convince him.

"Oh, well, if you say so, I guess it was," said Eishirou. "Huh, I really can't tell, though... By the way, Amagiri, are you going for the Japanese or the western option today?"

Ayato slumped his shoulders. "Fine. Take whatever you want."

"Heh-heh. I'll take the fish, then!"

At this rate, I'm on track to lose a dish from every meal. The fear crossed his mind, but Ayato told himself not to argue the point this time.

"Well, I'm going back to sleep. Good luck with your training!"

Ayato sighed. It felt like he had been sighing a lot more since coming to this school. And he was pretty sure that wasn't just a feeling.

*

"Hoo, man, am I sleepy. Morning, guys!" Yawning hugely, Eishirou opened the door to the classroom. He must have gone back to sleep, like he'd said, but apparently that was still insufficient for him.

Astonished, Ayato followed him in to find that most of the seats were already filled. Lively conversations bloomed here and there through the classroom like wildflowers, a scene no different from any other school. Whatever else one might say, the attendance rate looked respectable, so maybe the students here were serious about their studies after all.

"Good morning, Julis."

"…Oh. Hi."

When Ayato offered a greeting to the seat next to his, Julis threw back that curt reply, her chin still resting in her hand.

The din of the classroom paused all at once.

"Hey, did—did you just hear that?"

"Did the Princess just say hi to someone!?"

"We're not still dreaming, are we?"

"What kind of spell did that guy put on her?"

"Hold up—are we sure that's the real Julis?"

As her classmates erupted in a different kind of chatter, Julis slammed her hands on the desk and stood up. "Y-you're all unbelievably rude! Why can't I answer someone when they greet me!"

She made this statement with a look of consummate indignation, but the commotion showed no signs of quieting. Julis saying a word of greeting was beyond unexpected. That reaction revealed what kind of status she had in the class.

She could take the opportunity to break the ice with her classmates…

or maybe that's too much to hope for. As Ayato thought that, he remembered that he had only transferred in yesterday. It was all well and good to think of Julis, but he had to manage his own situation first.

Just then, Ayato noticed that the seat on his left, empty the day before, was occupied. A girl with beautiful bluish hair was sleeping soundly with her head flat on the desk.

Having two transfers in as many days seemed rather unlikely, so Ayato guessed that she had simply been absent yesterday.

He should introduce himself, he thought, but he didn't want to wake her up for it… Just as he was fretting about what to do, the girl blearily raised her head.

Yes! Great timing, he thought. "Hey, next-seat neighbor. Um, I just transferred here yesterday. I'm Ayato— Huh?"

He couldn't finish his introduction. As soon as he saw her face, he froze with a stunned look. "S-Saya?"

The girl stared blankly back at him, then tilted her head slightly and murmured, "Ayato…?"

"Whaaa—!? Saya, what're you doing here!?"

There was no mistake—it was Saya Sasamiya. As Ayato jumped out of his seat in surprise, Eishirou leaned in from behind with the gleaming eyes of a boy who has just found a new toy. "What's up? You two know each other?"

"Yeah, well… I guess you could say we're old friends. We sort of grew up together, I guess."

"Grew up together?" Eishirou dubiously looked back and forth between the two of them. "Then why didn't you know you'd both be students here?"

"Well, I mean we *sort of* grew up together, but we haven't seen each other since Saya moved abroad. It's been six years, I think."

"Huh… She doesn't seem to have much of a reaction, for her part," Eishirou remarked.

Saya was, in fact, staring at Ayato without the slightest change in expression.

"Um, well, that's true, but she's been like this for as long as I've known her. She *is* surprised. I think."

"Really?"

"Uh-huh," Saya mumbled. "I'm super surprised."

"Okay, but you don't really look it at all," Eishirou insisted weakly to Saya, who hadn't so much as moved an eyebrow.

"But it really has been a while. You're doing all right?" asked Ayato. She nodded once in reply.

"Just like always. You never change, Saya."

This time, Saya shook her head. "…That's not true. I'm taller."

"Oh… Are you?" Ayato looked more closely at his childhood friend, reunited with him entirely by coincidence.

She had a childish face, with adorably big eyes and an innocent shape. She didn't seem to have grown an inch since the day they'd last met—she could easily have passed for an elementary school student. Her expression hardly ever changed, giving her a charm best described (for better or worse) as doll-like.

"I don't think you've changed at all…"

"No. You just got too tall." Saya puffed out her cheeks in a pout. "…But that's all right. According to my estimates, by next year I should be about as tall as you are now. And you'll grow a little more, too, so the proportions will be just right."

Saya nodded in agreement with herself. But it was hard to imagine that she could grow by a foot in one year.

"But man, small world, huh?" said Eishirou. "A fateful reunion, I'd say."

"Fateful reunion… Yes. You put things nicely, Yabuki." Saya gave him a thumbs-up. Her readiness to go with the flow of things seemed unchanged as well.

"How about your dad and everyone? How are they doing?" Saya's father was a meteoric engineering scientist who had devoted his entire career to Lux development. Ayato recalled that her father's work was the reason for her family's move overseas.

"Almost too well. I wish he'd be more careful."

"Ha-ha. Sounds like he hasn't changed, either." The image of Saya's father that Ayato had in his head was the archetype of a mad scientist. He recalled that when he went over to the Sasamiyas' house to play as a child, he could hear Dr. Sasamiya cackling, holed up in his laboratory.

By reputation, he was an excellent scientist, but one with a difficult personality—owing to which he had changed employers several times.

"I'm here because my father told me to come."

"He did?"

Saya drew a Lux activator from the holster on her uniform. The grip-shaped activator turned on and a large automatic pistol materialized in an instant. The smooth flow of her movements hinted at her practiced hand. "He told me to advertise the gun he made."

"Advertising? *That's* why you're here?"

Even if the students weren't fighting to kill, Asterisk was not a safe place by any stretch of the imagination. Ayato could not have much esteem for the scientist's decision to send his own daughter here just to use her as publicity for a weapon.

"Eh, I don't think it's that crazy," Eishirou interjected. "If you make it to the big time here, that'd be better advertising than money could buy. I mean, that's half the reason the IEFs run this place, anyway."

"But are you okay with that, Saya?" Ayato fretted.

"I have my own reasons," she replied nonchalantly. "So I'm fine."

"Ah. Could you tell us more about those reasons?" Having shifted entirely into journalism mode, Eishirou had a serious look and a notepad in one hand.

"They're secret." Even as she said that, Saya glanced at Ayato. "But just now, one half of my reasons for coming here..."

"Ah-*ha*." That was all Eishirou needed, apparently, to understand the situation. "That reminds me, Sasamiya—you applied for an excursion permit as soon as you came here. Whatever happened with that?"

Asterisk was located within the country of Japan but had complete extraterritoriality. To leave Asterisk, one needed a legitimate purpose and the permission of one's school.

"...I haven't gotten it yet. What about it?"

"Oh, nothing. I was just wondering if maybe you didn't need it anym—" Grinning, Eishirou nearly finished the sentence before suddenly snapping his mouth shut. The muzzle of Saya's gun was pressing into his throat.

"…That's enough of your tactless conjectures."

"All right. Understood. Sorry. My bad." Eishirou held up both hands in surrender as Saya forced his chin upward, grinding it with the muzzle.

"I'm not sure what you're talking about," said Ayato, "but Saya's more violent than she looks, so be careful."

"You could've told me sooner…"

"Yo, sit your butts down. Time for homeroom." With that, Kyouko entered the class, looking lethargic. She didn't even hold up her nail bat, just dragged it across the floor, but the grating sound it made was sufficiently intimidating. "Hey, you, don't be swinging your piece around in my class… Oh, it's you, Sasamiya."

"Good morning, ma'am."

"Where the hell were you yesterday? Go on, I'm all ears." Kyouko stomped her way over to Saya, then crossed her arms and stared her down.

"…I just overslept."

"Ha-ha. I gotcha. You overslept." *Clonk.*

"…Ouch."

"You dumbass! How many times does that make!? The next day you miss'll land your little butt in make-up classes!"

Even after taking a fist to the head, Saya's face remained expressionless—except for the tiny hint of tears welling up in her eyes.

"Still not a morning person, huh?" said Ayato, laughing.

"…My bed always wins."

From her seat on the other side of Ayato, Julis watched the two of them, plainly unamused.

*

That same day, after school, Julis stood in front of the bathroom mirror.

"Well… Hmm. That should do it," she murmured to her reflection.

There was not a flaw to be seen in either her hair (which she honestly didn't care for herself, thinking it too showy) or her perfectly straightened uniform.

It's not as if I worry too much about how I look. It's a matter of etiquette, nothing more. Being less than circumspect with one's clothing leads to carelessness in other matters. I just told him something like that yesterday, after all, so I can't very well be negligent myself. Yes, that's it, Julis told herself, then headed back to the classroom.

There weren't many students left, but Ayato was in his seat, chatting happily with Saya.

Having overheard their conversation from this morning, Julis knew they had grown up together. *And now, they're seeing each other for the first time in years, so it's only natural that they have a lot to talk about,* she thought. But it still made her nervous for some reason.

"Um—*ahem.* Are you ready to go?"

"Oh. Hey, Julis. I appreciate this."

"W-well, I have to, don't I. A promise is a promise." Even as she curtly turned away from him, Julis was watching Ayato from the corner of her eye.

That easygoing, lackadaisical face of his. Suddenly she recalled that earnest look in his eyes when he'd saved her, and her heart beat faster. An emotion she didn't understand whirled in her chest, and she shook her head as if she could literally shake it off.

"…A promise?" asked Saya, mystified by their conversation.

"Julis is going to show me around campus today," Ayato explained.

"Riessfeld is? Why?"

"That's, um… Well, it's a long story," Julis replied. "Nothing to do with you, Sasamiya."

At that, Saya made a sulky noise, frowning faintly.

"Let's go," said Julis.

"Right. Okay, Saya, see you tom—"

"Wait. If that's all, Ayato, I'll show you around."

"*Wh—!?*"

"Huh?"

Julis and Ayato turned in surprise at this sudden declaration.

"I can give him a tour as well as anyone else," Saya went on. "You were saying you have to, Riessfeld. Like you don't want to. So, I can save you the trouble."

Now it was Julis who scowled. "The offer's appreciated. But I made a promise, and I don't break my promises."

"...But it would be better for Ayato, too, if the person showing him around actually wanted to."

"It—it's not that I don't *want* to! Anyway, you just started here yourself, Sasamiya! And I've been here since middle school. I think it's quite clear which one of us is more qualified."

Terrific sparks flew between them.

"Um, ladies...?" Ayato tried to intervene, but they didn't seem to hear him.

"Oh, if that's the issue at hand, I believe I would be most suited to the task."

Ayato let out a startled shout as Claudia poked her head in from behind him. She also had her arms around him, very deliberately pressing her ample bosom against his back.

As they took in the scene, Saya's and Julis's expressions respectively became even more intense.

"Julis came here for her third year of middle school," said Claudia, "while I matriculated properly back in year one."

"...Who are you?"

"Why are *you* here?"

"First of all, could you maybe give me a little space, Claudia!"

"Why, you're all so unfriendly. Since I'm here, I thought I might join in the fun..."

"...No."

"Request denied."

"Please, they're t-touching me!"

"Mm, how unfortunate. Well, then, I'll just finish my business here and be on my way." Claudia reluctantly let go of Ayato and held out a sheaf of papers for him. "Tomorrow, we'll select an Orga Lux for you and conduct a compatibility test, as we discussed earlier. Please look through these documents and make sure you have no objections to anything there before you sign."

"Oh—that." Tomorrow was sooner than Ayato would have liked, but this was his chance to see the Orga Lux that his sister might have wielded. He could not afford to miss it. "Okay. ...Wow, this is a ton of paperwork, though." There were at least ten different documents, all crammed with fine print.

"It's on loan to us, but it does belong to the IEF," said Claudia. "But that's all a formality, so please don't worry about it too much. Just skim right through it."

"If the president delivers paperwork like this herself, the student council must not have much to do," Julis remarked acidly.

Claudia brushed aside the insult. "Indeed, we don't—thanks to our students being so well-behaved."

"I was wondering this before," said Ayato, "but are you two friends?"

"Why, yes, we are."

"We certainly are not!"

Ayato tilted his head in confusion at the two polar opposite answers.

"Oh, how cold of you, Julis," Claudia mourned.

"We saw each other a few times at the Opernball in Vienna," Julis said flatly. "We're acquainted, no more and no less."

The Opernball was the largest society event in Europe, well known as the affair where young men and women of the upper classes made their debuts in high society.

"Now, if you're done here, why don't you get going," said Julis.

"Shoo, shoo," Saya added.

Claudia laughed softly. "Good day, then. But I'll have Ayato all to myself tomorrow. Don't think too ill of me."

With a single bow, she left, trailed by angry glares from Julis and Saya.

"That scheming vixen," muttered Julis. "Thinks she can do whatever she wants just because she's a little top-heavy... They're just bags of fat."

"...Agreed." Saya nodded vigorously.

They were so firmly on the same level that it was hard to believe they had been butting heads only moments ago. Eager to take the opportunity, Ayato hastily submitted a proposal for compromise. "Oh, I know! Since you're both here, maybe you can both show me around?"

"Both of us...?"

Julis and Saya looked at each other for a while, then laughed in resignation.

"...I accept."

"Very well. Let's not waste any more time arguing."

"*Whew.*" Looking profoundly relieved, Ayato wiped a drop of sweat from his brow.

And so the three of them toured the campus together.

"This is the club complex. Most of the clubs aren't all that active, but you might find yourself here if you have a complaint for one of the media clubs."

"...Mm-hmm."

"This is the Committee Center. You'll need to go through them for requests and adjustments for fringe benefits."

"...I see."

"And the dining halls—well, I suppose you must have found them by now. Anyway, there are seven places to eat on campus, including the cafeteria. But the one in the basement here is usually less crowded, so it's better to go there."

"...I didn't know that."

"Sasamiya, you do understand that I'm not giving *you* a tour?" said Julis, as the three of them took a break on a courtyard bench.

Saya had been carefully taking in all the details of Julis's campus tour. "...I have no sense of direction."

"I'm amazed you would offer to show someone else around," Julis sniffed.

Saya coughed humbly.

"That wasn't a compliment."

"Oh, it's okay," said Ayato with his usual carefree smile. "I learned a lot, too. Really, thank you."

"W-well, all right, but..."

"I know, I'll go get us something to drink. What'll you have? My treat."

"Hmm. Iced tea, then."

"I'll have apple juice. Not from concentrate, hopefully."

"Got it." Ayato took off, making his way around the sizable fountain and back toward the high school building.

Actually, the vending machines at the middle school building are closer, thought Julis. *I'll have to show him later...*

As Julis smiled wryly to herself, Saya interrupted her musings. "...Riessfeld, there's something I still want to know."

"What?"

"Why did you promise to show Ayato around?"

"You're persistent, I'll give you that... Fine, I'll tell you. It's because I owed him a debt. That's all it is."

"What debt was that?"

Julis hesitated for a moment but reluctantly told her the truth. "He saved me from an outside attack during a duel."

"A duel? Riessfeld, you dueled Ayato?"

"Yes. You didn't hear?"

Duels by Page One students were always fodder for gossip, and Julis was sure that videos of it must have made the news last night. Apparently, this particular classmate of hers wasn't interested in the rankings.

"But I'm not going to tell you why we dueled," said Julis. "That's a private matter."

"...Who won?"

"There was some interference. The duel was declared void."

"...That's funny."

"What is?"

"If you really fought Ayato, you shouldn't be in one piece."

The unexpected remark caught Julis off guard. She wondered if Saya was joking, but her eyes were quite serious.

"You must not have a very high opinion of me."

"You're strong, Riessfeld. I know that," Saya told her, calm and straightforward. "But on the same level as me, at best. And that's no match for Ayato."

Hearing that, laid out as if it were such an obvious truth, Julis felt her heart clench.

"Oh?" she retorted. "That's a bold statement."

The air tensed like a string drawn taut.

To the best of her knowledge, Saya's name was not among the Named Chart. And Julis kept track of the other strong students in her class. Never talking to others much, she couldn't be sure, but she didn't think Saya had even participated in the official ranking matches.

Of course, rankings were not the sole indicator of strength. Julis herself had said as much to Ayato earlier. And there were more than a few students who disliked attention enough to keep their abilities hidden until just before the Festa.

Whatever the case, this was not an insult Julis could overlook.

"Very well. Care to try me?"

Without a word, Saya stood up and placed some distance between them.

Julis, interpreting this as assent, stood and placed her hand on her school crest.

"I, Julis-Alexia von Riessfeld, challenge thee, Saya Sasamiya, to—" Julis began but instinctively leaped back.

Not half a second later, there was a light dry sound as several arrows of light flew one after another into the bench.

It was a side attack. So, not from Saya, but—

"The fountain!?" How long the person had been there, Julis had no idea, but a sharpshooter dressed in black stood waist-deep in the water, holding a crossbow-shaped Lux. "Hmph. Another ambush?"

Most likely the same culprit as last time, she thought. With a mocking laugh, Julis focused her prana and called forth the fire from within.

"Burst into bloom—*Longiflorum!*" She generated the spear of fire midair and released it as she landed.

It was a perfectly timed counterattack, but the blazing spear that should have impaled her target was intercepted by a dark shadow that leaped into its path.

"Another one…! But—someone able to ward off my flames…?"

Like the sniper, the newcomer was also clad in black. The giant ax-shaped Lux he wielded with both hands must have served as a shield.

Judging from their shared lack of sartorial judgment, they had to be working together. The one that had been hiding in the fountain was rather squat, while the second one was a muscular giant of a man, well over six feet tall.

That physique and choice of weapon reminded her of someone—but this was no time to figure out whom. Considering how well they hid their presence, these were not enemies to be taken lightly. Julis could get all the answers she needed out of them after beating them down.

But just as she was about to focus her prana to attack—

"...*Boom.*"

And the giant went flying sideways with an earthshaking explosion. He went some forty or fifty feet before falling to the ground in a tailspin, then lay completely motionless.

"Wha...?" Bracing herself against the wind from the blast, Julis was dumbfounded to see Saya with an enormous gun, larger than her own stature. It was hard to say, actually, whether Saya was holding the gun or whether she was an attachment to it.

"What is *that*?"

"Type thirty-eight Lux grenade launcher, Helnekraum."

"You mean it shoots *grenades*...?"

Saya nodded and casually trained the muzzle on the fountain. "...*Burst.*" The gun glowed faintly. Her prana rose dramatically and poured into the huge gun, and the manadite shone even more brightly. This could only be...

"Meteor Arts!?"

The stocky attacker was scrambling out of the fountain, trying to get away—too late.

"...*Kaboom.*" Released with a murmur rather than a shout from Saya, the projectile of light exploded at the moment of contact with its target.

A deafening roar sounded and the fountain was completely obliterated. Water gushed up from the base to rain down on the surroundings like an oversized shower.

The scale of the explosion might be comparable to her Amaryllis,

Julis thought, but this was superior in pure destructive power. "You are more violent than you look."

"...Not as much as you, Riessfeld."

Julis had no rejoinder for that.

"I'm not going to thank you," she said instead. "I could have handled them myself." The attackers were skilled, yes, but she was confident in her ability to drive them off.

"No need. They were just in our way," Saya replied in her usual blunt manner, then turned to Julis. "...Shall we continue?"

Julis was confused for a moment, then nearly burst into laughter when she realized that Saya meant their duel. "No, I'll pass. You really are strong. I apologize for underestimating you."

"...Okay, then." As easily as that, Saya deactivated her Lux.

I'm probably not one to talk, Julis thought, *but this girl's an odd one, too.*

"Well, then, shall we hand over these miscreants to the disciplinary committee?"

As if on cue, a black-clad figure emerged from underneath the rubble, pushing his way out of the wreckage. Julis and Saya promptly took combat stances again, but the surprisingly nimble attacker was already disappearing into the woods. Then they noticed that the giant was gone, too.

"Hardy, aren't they?" said Julis.

"...I'm amazed."

From the force of that impact, an ordinary opponent would have had difficulty even moving.

"Well, there's not much we can do now that they've gotten away. If we chase them without being careful, we might fall into a trap. Anyway, Sasamiya, you destroyed school property. You should report it."

"...Me?"

"Yes, you. You blew up the fountain."

"...Too much trouble. I'll leave it to you, Riessfeld."

"Why *me*? This is serious."

"Hey!" As the two of them went back and forth, Ayato came running from the direction of the high school buildings. "I heard this huge noise and... Wait, whoa—! What happened here!?" he exclaimed, seeing the pulverized fountain.

"Well, something came up. Right, Sasamiya?"

"...Yes. Something came up."

This wasn't much of an explanation. But neither of them particularly wanted to go through the trouble of explaining from the beginning. So they left it at that.

"I'm not sure what happened, but... *Augh!*" Ayato was looking around, puzzled, when his face suddenly went scarlet and he stared awkwardly off to the side.

Julis cocked her head at him—and immediately understood.

Everything nearby was completely soaked with the water spraying from the ruins of the fountain. Julis and Saya were no exception. This resulted in the thin fabric of their summer uniforms clinging closely to their skin and, of course, becoming entirely translucent.

In a panic, Julis looked down to see that her undergarments showed clearly through.

"Wha—? You—d-don't you dare look! You'll pay if you open your eyes!"

"I'm not looking! Not looking!"

"Hmm, see-through. How very erotic."

"Ugh, Sasamiya! Cover your shame! Wait—wh-why aren't you wearing a bra?" Julis's eyes widened in surprise as she turned to look at Saya, whose uniform also clung tight to her body.

Both of them were equally soaked through—but there was one fatal difference.

"...It's sad to say, but I don't need one yet."

At Saya's utterly unruffled tone, Julis clutched her head in dismay. "Anyway—go get us something to cover up! Now!"

"Uh—right!"

It was only a matter of time before the commotion of a fountain getting blown up compelled all the gawking idiot students of Seidoukan Academy to gather.

As she watched Ayato run off, Julis heaved a terrific sigh.

CHAPTER 5
THE SER VERESTA

The next day, Ayato went to the student council office to see about the Orga Lux compatibility test. Claudia greeted him with a smile.

"I heard what happened yesterday, Ayato."

The news that Julis was attacked again had been reported to the disciplinary committee on the same day. Naturally, Claudia had learned of it as well.

The story was also making the rounds on the Net news, but every feature spoke of "Julis repelling mysterious attackers." There was no mention of Saya's name or even the fact that someone else had been there. It would seem that Page One students received different treatment than their unranked peers did.

Well, the way things work here is plain enough, thought Ayato.

"Do you think the attackers will be caught?" he asked.

"Hmm—to be honest, I'm not very optimistic," she replied. "We've asked the disciplinary committee to conduct a full investigation, but there's not much evidence to speak of."

"Even in Asterisk, that's obviously a crime, isn't it? Shouldn't the police be taking care of it?"

The disciplinary committee was, after all, only a student organization. An investigative body with official authority had to be better suited to the task.

"That's the sticky part," said Claudia. "There is an organization in

Asterisk that acts as the police force—the Stjarnagarm. But they're too good at their jobs."

"What do you mean?"

"Their jurisdiction is limited to the urban area of Asterisk, not extending to the properties of the six schools—at least, that's how all of the schools interpret the law. The schools don't allow them on campus except in extreme circumstances."

The opinion of the schools was the opinion of the integrated enterprise foundations, and the latter was law in Asterisk. Which meant that so long as the schools didn't allow it, even this so-called Stjarnagarm couldn't set a single foot on campus.

"I guess you wouldn't want them poking around where it doesn't hurt," said Ayato.

"We don't want them poking around precisely because it would hurt," Claudia admitted matter-of-factly. "If it were up to me, I would ask for their help. But in this case, my authority has little weight. If only Julis were more cooperative, we might have more options at our disposal…"

"Geez. I don't know why she's so stubborn."

After reporting the incident to the disciplinary committee, Julis rejected any further involvement. She was adamant that she needed help from no one. The committee even offered a personal security team, but Julis turned them down flat: "Bodyguards who are weaker than me would hardly be any help."

"That girl is probably doing all she can to protect what she's holding in her hands," said Claudia. "Maybe she thinks that if she tries to grasp something else, she'll drop what she has now."

"Holding…in her hands…?"

"Well, that's a different subject altogether. In any case, I can't overlook this matter. Which is why I wanted to ask you a favor—" As Claudia leaned forward, a sharp rapping at the door came. "Oh, I do apologize. I forgot that we were expecting another visitor. We'll continue this later."

Claudia operated the controls at her desk, and the door opened to let in a group that Ayato was not expecting. The feeling was mutual, as the newcomers all looked at him with surprised faces.

"Applying for Orga Lux usage is a rather cumbersome process, so I wanted to get it done in one go if possible. Now, let me introduce you..." Her friendly offer of introductions was, in fact, completely unnecessary.

The visitors were none other than Lester and his sidekicks.

Claudia quickly noticed the tension and tilted her head curiously. "Oh, are you already acquainted, by any chance?"

"Well, in a manner of speaking," Ayato muttered.

"Wh-what are *you* doing here?" Randy, the pudgy one, pointed at Ayato, slack-jawed.

As for Lester, he shot one irritated glance at Ayato and avoided further eye contact.

"I'll have Ayato and Mr. MacPhail both take the compatibility test today. The two of you," she said, addressing the sidekicks, "cannot enter the vault—as I believe you're aware. Is that clear?"

"Oh. Yes, of course." The thin one, Silas, nodded.

"Let's get this started already," Lester growled. "I don't have all day."

Claudia chuckled softly. "So impatient. But I agree that we should use our time efficiently. Shall we, then?" She stood up and led the way out of the student council office.

As they walked down the gleaming hallway, Ayato asked Claudia the question that had been on his mind for a while. "So what *is* the procedure for taking out an Orga Lux?"

"Oh, the procedure itself is simple. We measure your compatibility rating with the Orga Lux of your choice, and if it exceeds eighty percent, it is lent out to you."

"That's it?"

"Yes."

That seemed anticlimactic. The urm-manadite crystals in Orga Lux cores were said to have value beyond any sum of money. Ayato wondered if it made much sense to lend out such objects to students so lightly.

"Heh. You don't know a damn thing," Lester jeered, close behind Ayato. "Being entrusted with an Orga Lux is easier said than done. Not just anybody can apply, to start with. You have to be highly ranked or fight well at a Festa...or be on a special scholarship. And *then* you better hope you're lucky enough to come across an Orga Lux with a compatibility rating above eighty percent. And even if you are allowed to use one, whether you can wield it well is a whole other question."

The compatibility rating was an estimate for how well an individual could draw out an Orga Lux's power. Unlike ordinary Luxes, which could be activated and controlled by anyone, Orga Luxes were finicky and harder to handle.

Urm-manadite was manadite of extraordinary purity able to generate, to some extent, special powers similar to those of Stregas and Dantes. The compatibility rating test served as a measure of whether a user could fully wield those powers. In the end, it came down to individual suitability, and no amount of effort on the part of the user could change the basic value.

"Considering that you're trying for the third time, your words do carry some weight," Claudia remarked.

Lester had been speaking boastfully, but at that, he scowled and spat, "I'll get it this time."

"Yeah, Lester! You were just unlucky before," Randy piped up. "You'll make it this time for sure!"

"Heh. Course I will."

The flattery seemed a little forced, but it was enough to restore Lester's mood.

"So you can try as many times as you want?" asked Ayato.

"With permission, yes," said Claudia. "It does little good for the school to let an Orga Lux sit unused. Although it's still true that the vetting process is strict—unless you happen to be a Page One."

That is *quite a perk*, thought Ayato.

"Still, even Page One privileges have their limits. Further applications can be denied if a candidate is deemed unlikely to find a match."

Before long they arrived at the Matériel Department, located beneath the high school building—underwater, to be precise, since Asterisk was an artificial island. But with no windows to be seen, this made little practical difference.

As Ayato looked around curiously, walking down a corridor with people in lab coats who looked like the department staff, a faint voice suddenly spoke from behind him.

"H-hey. Sorry about the other day."

He turned to see Silas standing there with a timid smile.

"Lester isn't a bad guy, but, uh…he can be a bit temperamental…" Silas bowed his head in apology, looking abashed.

"Oh—no, it's fine," said Ayato.

"And Randy just goes along with him, you know, so the two of them might give you trouble later… I'm really sorry. Yesterday, they were talking, and it sounded like—"

"Hey, Silas! What the hell are you doing!?"

"Yeah, get over here!"

Lester and Randy were shouting at him from up ahead.

"Y—yes, sir!" Silas bowed to Ayato once more, then hurried to catch up to the other two boys.

It was clear that among the three of them, Lester occupied the top of the hierarchy and Silas was at the bottom. "Hmm," Ayato mumbled, taking this in.

Deep in the back of the Matériel Department, there was an elevator, which took them farther down. Finally they came to an open space that looked like a training arena. For all that they were underground, the ceiling was quite high.

One wall was covered with a hexagonal pattern, and part of the opposite wall was a large glass window. Beyond the glass were several busy men and women in lab coats, who, judging from their apparent age, were not students, but employees of the department. Randy and Silas stood with them, watching.

"I'm going first," said Lester. "Any problems?"

"What do you think, Ayato?" asked Claudia.

"Oh, um, sure. Go ahead."

Ayato simply wanted to see the Orga Lux that his sister had (or might have) used. It didn't matter to him who attempted the test first.

With a practiced hand, Lester manipulated the control panel at the edge of the wall with the hexagons. A number of enormous air-windows popped open, and he peered at them in grim deliberation.

Ayato looked on from a short distance back. "What's all that?" he murmured to Claudia, who stood next to him.

"It's a catalog of the Orga Luxes in the possession of Seidoukan Academy. The number currently stands at twenty-two. That's the most among the six schools."

"Wow."

"The catalog lists the type of weapon, along with its name and power. Please pick the one you would like to be tested for. Those appearing in gray are currently in use by another student—that is, they're already checked out."

"So that means, um…" Ayato began counting the ones displayed in gray.

"There are seven students currently using Orga Luxes," said Claudia with a laugh. "Of those, four are Page One."

A third of the Page One students were Orga Lux users. That alone was an indication of how powerful these weapons were.

"All right. This one." Lester selected a weapon from the catalog and closed the windows.

At the same time, one of the hexagonal markings began to glow, switching places one after the other with the adjacent hexagons, until the shining outline came smoothly to where Lester was standing. Finally, with a low rumble, the hexagon protruded from the wall. What appeared to be patterns on the wall were storage cases.

"Such a silly precaution," Claudia laughed.

"Silly…?" Ayato felt bad for the people who designed the storage system, only for the student council president to make fun of it.

"Oh?" Claudia raised her eyebrows. "Mr. MacPhail—you chose the Ser Veresta, the Blade of the Black Furnace? Now, that is interesting…"

"Ser Veresta?" Ayato repeated.

"Yes, an Orga Lux so powerful it was feared by the other schools— 'All it touches shall melt, and the earth so impaled shall be as a crucible.'"

"That...sounds a little overdramatic."

"It does have the power to live up to such a description. Well, that's beside the point. The thing is..." Claudia paused with an uncomfortable smile. "*That* is the Orga Lux whose records may have been altered."

"What!?"

Lester took the activator from the case, then strode to the middle of the arena and gave a signal toward the window.

Ayato fixed his gaze on the object in Lester's hand. "So that's it... the one my sister might have used."

In appearance, it was hardly any different from an ordinary Lux activator. The only distinction he could have named was the color of the manadite core. The manadite used in Luxes was always green, but urm-manadite came in a variety of colors. The core of the activator in Lester's hand glittered a bright red.

"Time to get started!" Lester switched on the activator and the hilt began to materialize, quite large in itself. Without pause, the hilt opened and a shining blade emerged.

Counter to its epithet of "Blade of the Black Furnace," the sword was an almost translucent, pure white. It seemed like a giant sword of light, apparently single edged.

As Ayato leaned in for a better look, his heart jumped with a single violent beat. A shudder went through him as if he had locked eyes with an unknowable monster. The sensation lasted only a moment—then it was gone.

What was that...? As Ayato tried to make sense of it, a voice rang out from speakers overhead.

"Calibrations complete. Please begin."

On cue, Lester let out a roar with the Ser Veresta in his hands. *"Yaaaaaargh!"*

Ayato could tell that Lester's prana was rising ferociously, but there was no corresponding energy from the Ser Veresta.

"Your current compatibility rating is thirty-two percent."

Lester went red with fury at the announcement. "I'm not done yet—!" he howled, the muscles in his arms bulging from the force of his grip, his teeth clenching so hard they might crack. He was the very embodiment of a will to suppress anything in his way with sheer overwhelming might.

But the Ser Veresta seemed to take no notice. Then it let out a sudden, vicious flash of light and sent Lester's large frame flying. He shouted in pain and frustration.

The Ser Veresta lingered in midair—Ayato wasn't sure how—and seemed to look down on Lester. As if it had just swatted away a noisy, annoying insect.

"It rejected him," Claudia murmured.

"So this is what they mean when they say that Orga Luxes have wills of their own…"

"That's right. We have no way of communicating with them, and yet…"

"Your comprehensive reading is twenty-eight percent," said the voice from the speakers.

"This isn't over!" Thrown to the wall, Lester stood up, undaunted, and took hold of the Ser Veresta again.

"I don't have a problem with that sort of…bullheaded pursuit of strength," said Claudia, "but I doubt that he's going to win the sword over by force."

"You can tell all that?"

"Well, I am an Orga Lux user myself."

This was news to Ayato.

"Mr. MacPhail also chose an Orga Lux of note in his previous attempt and the time before that. Those tests went much the same way. It's possible that they can see through his simple desire to have any weapon as long as it is powerful. I don't think that's such a terrible modus operandi, but…" Claudia trailed off and looked toward Lester.

He seemed to be trying to impose his will on the Ser Veresta. Each attempt only ended with him getting flung to the wall. "Damn it! Why!? Why won't you *obey*!?"

"It doesn't seem to care for his attitude. But I suppose that's hardly surprising, given its reputation for being hard to please."

"Really?"

"It's a relatively old Orga Lux, but there have only been two students who were ever able to wield it—oh, three, if you include *her.*"

"My sister used that sword..."

By now Lester was unable to even touch the Ser Veresta. It knocked him back just for getting close.

"Your compatibility rating is seventeen percent."

As his numbers fell, Lester made no attempt to hide his frustration. "Just do as I say, damn it!" As he tried to grab the sword with a fierce yell, he was knocked back harder than ever. Slammed hard against the wall, he slumped to his knees in defeat with a furious grunt.

"Your compatibility rating has shifted negative! It's not safe to continue the test. We must ask you to stop!"

"Oh, this isn't good. It seems to be seriously offended now." Sounding uncharacteristically nervous, Claudia took a step forward, but then came to a dead stop. Ayato immediately understood why. The Ser Veresta, still floating in the air, was emanating an intense heat. It was like being grilled by an open flame, even from ten yards or so away.

"The subject is out of control! Please evacuate immediately!" the panicked voice rang out from the speakers. *"Subject's heat output is rapidly climbing!"*

That last part was unnecessary for Ayato and Claudia, who could feel it for themselves. They were on the verge of being roasted alive.

"That sword is supposed to store heat within its blade," Claudia explained. "Now there's no one to control it, so the heat seems to be leaking out a little."

"Does this sort of thing happen a lot?"

"An Orga Lux running out of control? No. I've come across a few records of it, but this is the first time I've seen it happen. Shall we run?"

"I'd absolutely love to, but..." The room already felt like a sauna.

As sweat poured down his skin, Ayato could feel it—the Ser Veresta was watching him.

And its blade was lowered to point straight at him.

For some reason, it was targeting him.

If it were a person, he might have tried to talk his way out, but he was facing a sword. He doubted he could distract it with banter.

"I guess I have no choice," he sighed.

With his eyes fixed on the point of the blade, he focused his prana. Doing so sent a dull pain shooting all over his body, but he couldn't let that slow him down.

The Ser Veresta seemed to return Ayato's gaze, then rushed at him.

The blade flew at him with savage speed. Ayato dodged it by a hair's breadth, and even as he winced at its extraordinary heat, he reached out toward the grip. But the moment he tried to wrap his fingers around it, the Ser Veresta flipped in the air and sliced at his chest.

Ayato sprang out of the way, but not before his uniform had been sliced open by the searing edge. "Can I get reimbursed for this?"

"Hey!" For a second, Ayato thought Lester was admonishing him for the blasé one-liner, but he quickly saw that Lester meant to warn him.

In a flash, the Ser Veresta flew to the ceiling and then lunged straight down toward Ayato. The attack came precisely from his blind spot, but Ayato twisted, like he knew it was coming. As the Ser Veresta shot past him, he grabbed the hilt as if it were an animal's tail.

"Ouch!" For all that he was expecting it, the grip was unbearably hot. He could feel his flesh burning even as he focused his prana to protect the palm of his hand.

Still, Ayato did not loosen his hold. In a single motion, he drove the Ser Veresta's blade into the floor. "Sorry, but I don't like people chasing after me—the same as you."

That same instant, the heat that had filled the room vanished. The Ser Veresta, too, came to a complete stop—almost as if nothing had happened. Ayato let out a sigh of relief.

As everyone else looked on in awed silence, Claudia alone applauded him. "Very impressive, Ayato. Well done. Do you have a reading for his compatibility rating?"

The department staff stood frozen in shock for a few moments before realizing that Claudia had addressed them. They snapped to attention and someone reported, *"N-ninety-seven percent!"*

"Thank you." Claudia nodded in satisfaction, then turned to Lester. "You heard the numbers. It's an unfortunate outcome for you, but I trust that you have no objections?"

Lester stared at Ayato, still unable to believe what he'd seen. Finally he bit his lip in frustration and slammed his fist against the floor.

*

"There. All done." Claudia gently released Ayato's right hand, having applied ointment and bandages to his burns. "But are you sure you won't go to the campus infirmary? They'll be able to treat you more properly."

"No, this is just fine. Thank you." Ayato made a fist and there was hardly any pain. It did sting a little, but that was only to be expected.

"All right, if you say so…"

Ayato and Claudia were once again in the student council room. She had practically dragged him in here to bandage him up, since he had burned his hand grabbing the Ser Veresta.

They sat side by side on the sofa. For some reason she was leaning in very close, which flustered him, but he asked her something that had been on his mind. "Is it really okay for me to use it?"

After that commotion, the Ser Veresta was officially placed into Ayato's care. The registration process would take two or three more days, though, and the sword was not in his possession yet.

"No one would object to a ninety-seven percent compatibility rating. Would you prefer something other than the Ser Veresta?"

"No—it's the sword my sister might have used, so I was curious about it. It's just that, well…"

"Is it about Mr. MacPhail?"

Ayato nodded, remembering Lester's inordinately frustrated look when they left. "I just feel bad that I kind of ended up taking the sword away from him."

"That's simply the way things go. Competition is the very nature of this city. Which is not to say that there's no place for friendship and cooperation, but one has to accept it when someone else comes out on top."

"I hope Lester sees it that way, too." Ever since their first meeting, Ayato had the feeling that the other student didn't think too well of him.

"Did something happen between the two of you?"

"Well, technically, it was with him and Julis, not me..." Ayato explained the exchange between Lester and Julis from the previous afternoon.

"Ah... Mr. MacPhail's obsession with Julis is well known."

"I can't do anything about it if Lester has a grudge against me," said Ayato. "But with what happened to Julis yesterday—I don't want it to cause more trouble for her."

"Do you think that Mr. MacPhail is the one who attacked Julis?"

Ayato smiled awkwardly at the probing question. "I didn't say that... Sure, the guy who attacked Julis yesterday was as big as Lester, but it's not fair to treat him like a suspect just based on that."

"But wouldn't you agree that he has the motive? It's a widely known fact that he harbors less than friendly feelings toward her after losing to her repeatedly."

"That's why I think it's *not* him. Lester doesn't exactly have a grudge against Julis—he just wants to beat her or maybe just get her to admit that he's strong. So there's no point in him sneaking around sniping at her. I think that when the time comes, he wants to challenge her head-on, in front of plenty of witnesses."

"Then why do you think that what happened today might cause trouble for Julis?"

"Whoever is behind the attacks seems to be carefully choosing their opportunities. Well, I guess that's only natural—Julis is strong, and there's a good chance they can't take her in a fair fight. But if she's already fighting, even someone as strong as Julis has to concentrate on the opponent in front of her."

"Which is the perfect chance for them to strike."

"It was the same when she dueled me, and yesterday, she was attacked just as she was about to duel Saya. I was worried that if Lester has even more incentive to fight Julis, that could put her in danger."

"I see... That's very insightful." Claudia nodded, looking impressed.

She looked just like a teacher praising a student who'd done well, and Ayato was convinced the comparison wasn't far off. *She probably figured all of this out already.*

Just as he thought that, Claudia sat up straighter and turned to face him.

"Ayato, I'd like to ask a favor of you. I'm certain that you're the right person for the task. Could you meet me tonight?"

"Huh? Sure, but—can't you ask me now?"

"No. This demands a certain level of secrecy. I'll contact you later about the exact time and place."

It seemed odd to Ayato that she would insist on secrecy when there were only the two of them in the room.

"They say the walls have ears and the doors have eyes," Claudia went on, as if she'd read his mind. "This place is a maelstrom of schemes and trickery. It's not as safe as you might think."

That night, when it was almost lights-out for the dormitories, Ayato finally received a call on his mobile. He didn't want Eishirou to hear, so he put the call on hold and left the dorm. Luckily for him, there was no curfew here for high school students.

"I apologize for calling so late. I had to attend a meeting after our earlier talk." There were no air-windows. She had made a voice-only call.

"It's fine for me. But isn't it a little late for you?" Even though there was no curfew, this was not an hour when girls walked alone outside.

"A little bit. So I was hoping that I could ask you to come here."

"Where's 'here'?"

"My room."

"Your room, as in, in the girls' dorm?"

"Yes. I'm on the top floor on the southeast side. I'll leave the window open, so just come in that way," she said as if this would be completely normal.

"Um, I actually got into huge trouble for doing that earlier…" The last time, he hadn't known that it was a girls-only dormitory. He wouldn't have the excuse of ignorance now.

"Don't worry. Unlike Julis, I won't challenge you to a duel."

"I think you might be missing the point." The student council president breaking the rules could only set a problematic example.

"I'll be waiting."

"Hey—just a minute! Claudia!?"

She had already hung up on him. And she didn't pick up when he tried to call back. Ayato felt an urge to curl up with his face in his hands, but he couldn't just pretend that he hadn't heard her.

Sometimes it's hard to tell what she really wants, but Claudia is someone I can trust… I think.

Resigned, Ayato decided to head to the girls' dormitory. "If Julis sees me, I'm dead for sure this time…"

At first glance, the building would seem to be light on security, but there was a reason for that. The girls' dormitory at Seidoukan Academy placed its emphasis less on preventing intruders than on driving them away by force.

Ordinary security measures were insufficient to ward off Genestella. On the other hand, security that was too tight would pose an inconvenience to the students who lived there. The girls' dormitory solved this dilemma by improving the communication system for the dormitory watch.

Students in the dormitory could raise the alarm with a single word or a push of a button. The system was highly customizable—for example, one student might set an alarm to alert the dormitory watch if the window in her room was broken, and an extremely cautious student might set the alarm to sound if anyone other than herself entered her room.

Thus alerted, the dormitory watch took an average of two minutes to arrive on the scene and mete out swift and merciless justice on the intruder—no questions asked, no excuses heard.

When he'd heard about this security system, Ayato couldn't help but be thankful that the incident from the other morning had not turned out much worse. If Julis had set her alarm options differently, Ayato could have been the target of that justice. But he had also heard that Julis turned most of her alarm settings to OFF, probably due to a confidence that she could ward off intruders without any help from the dormitory watch.

"Okay, there's Claudia's room," Ayato said to himself, arriving at the dorm. "There are footholds, so it'll be easier than before, but this really does make me look like a degenerate..."

He moved closer, trying to keep out of sight, then made use of the scarce footholds to carefully make his way up to the top story. Flattening himself against the wall like a gecko, he edged his way to the room.

He knocked lightly on the window and found it unlocked, just as Claudia had said.

A possible flaw with this security setup was that students could invite in anyone if they so wished. One had to wonder what this meant with respect to appropriate conduct for students their age, but the dormitory watch was apparently not in the business of involving itself in students' private affairs.

"Claudia? I'm coming in," Ayato called. There was no response.

It wasn't easy to keep clinging to the outside wall like that, so he timidly stepped into the room.

The place was stylishly decorated and far larger than the room he shared with Eishirou, more like a suite in a luxury hotel than a dorm room. The furnishings were tasteful down to the tiniest accessory, reflecting the aesthetic sense of its occupant.

That occupant, however, was nowhere to be seen. "She couldn't possibly be out...," he murmured.

There was another room, probably the bedroom. Could she be in there? Just as Ayato was about to reluctantly peek in, the door at the far side of the room opened with a *clack*.

"Oh, you're already here. Forgive me—I was in the shower."

Ayato had no words. Claudia was cloaked in clouds of rising steam. Other than that, she was clad in no more than a single bath towel and that only loosely wrapped around her torso. Her generous breasts seemed as though they might pop out at any moment. The towel was too small for her curves, exposing her supple thighs to a brazen extent. Her flushed skin only added to her already excessive womanly charm.

"I'll get dressed. Please make yourself at home." Drops of water glistening in her wet hair, Claudia calmly walked across to the bed-room, passing right in front of the petrified Ayato.

How am I supposed to feel at home in this situation!? Ayato wanted to shout, but considering that he was the one who'd snuck in, he couldn't say much. At that moment, it was doubtful that his voice would have worked anyway.

"Sorry to keep you waiting," she called out after a bit. "Come this way, would you?"

"......Okay." Ayato followed her voice into the bedroom.

Claudia sat on the bed, now draped in only a bathrobe, which Ayato might have expected.

"You're...maybe a little too relaxed," he remarked.

"I'm always like this at home."

Ayato didn't know where to look. But anything he said about it would fall on deaf ears.

As he sat down on the sofa with a sigh, Claudia poured a ruby-colored liquid into a glass she had ready. "There's plenty for you, too. Would you like some?"

"I'm better off not asking what that is, right?"

"That's very wise of you," she said with a giggle.

Ayato politely declined. "Your room is pretty huge. Is this one of the perks of being student council president?" he asked, looking around the room—and doing his best not to look at her.

"No, this has more to do with being a highly ranked fighter than my position as president. Page One students are given rooms like this one, as well as special treatment in financial matters."

"Oh, you're a Page One, too, Claudia?"

Claudia gave him a forlorn smile. "Why, Ayato, you're so cruel. You might show a *little* more interest in me."

"S-sorry."

"Well, never mind that. At any rate, being student council president is a lot of trouble without much in return."

"Then why did you agree to be president?"

"Because I like trouble." She laughed enigmatically and gracefully recrossed her legs. Even as her enthralling thighs beckoned to his glance, Ayato made an effort to look away and get to the point.

"So...does the favor you wanted to ask me have to do with that sort of trouble?"

"I'm glad you're so astute. Take a look at this, please." Claudia touched her mobile device and several air-windows popped open. Each one showed a different student, with little apparently in common.

"All of these students were registered for the upcoming Phoenix Festa. There are no Page Ones among them, but they're all ranked fairly high in the Named Chart. And they were all expected to do well."

"You're speaking in the past tense."

"Exactly. Every one of these students had to withdraw recently due to injury," Claudia said with a sigh and closed the windows.

"All for different reasons. An accident here, a dueling wound there... Injuries are fairly commonplace in this city, to some degree. That's one reason why it took us so long to notice. But upon further inspection, we found something suspicious about the circumstances in each case."

"You think a third party was involved? Like with Julis?"

"Yes. There are no reports that they were targets of direct attacks. But when you were dueling Julis, they used a sniper, keeping themselves hidden. It's very likely that in these other cases, too, the attackers never showed themselves."

Ayato sat for a moment in thought. "Do you have any evidence?"

"No, none. And the students who were attacked wouldn't cooperate with the investigation."

"What do you mean?"

"Well…it's a problem unique to this school, or rather, to Genestella. Students who have some confidence in their abilities have a tendency to reject the help of others. There was even one who wanted to go after the culprits alone as soon as their injuries healed."

"I see. That is a problem…"

"They might respond differently if we could explain everything— but we can't exactly do that, either."

They wanted to handle things themselves exactly *because* they could handle themselves in a fight, Ayato thought. Of course, there were some students who would have let the disciplinary committee help. But if the attackers had targeted students with a certain type of personality, they had planned things carefully.

"This is just between us, but the disciplinary committee is looking into Lester MacPhail as a probable suspect," said Claudia. "He and Randy Hooke have no alibi for the time of the attack on Julis yesterday."

"But you think that's right, do you?"

"No. The same as you." Claudia smiled brightly.

"So Silas isn't a suspect? I got the impression that the three of them were always together."

"Silas Norman has a flawless alibi. His roommate and his friends all say that he was in his room studying at the time of the attack."

"Oh… Well, anyway, with so few clues to go on, we can't be very proactive."

"You're right. But we do have one thing in our favor," Claudia said, raising her index finger. "We know who their next target is."

"…Julis."

"Yes. If they were willing to attack just anyone, they wouldn't risk being seen. And they wouldn't go so far as to target a Page One. This means that whoever is responsible is going after powerful students, fully aware of how difficult their task is. From this, we can speculate…" Ayato leaned in to listen. "…That they're working for one of the other schools."

"Another school is involved?"

"Yes, and the culprit is one of our own students. Most of the attacks took place on our campus, and it would be too risky for students of another school to infiltrate."

"But that would be..."

The six schools that vied for supremacy in Asterisk—Seidoukan Academy, Saint Gallardworth Academy, Le Wolfe Black Institute, Jie Long Seventh Institute, Allekant Académie, and Queenvale Academy for Young Ladies—were not exactly on friendly terms with each other.

It's only natural given that they're all in competition, Ayato thought. *But isn't this going outside the law?*

"Of course, such conduct cannot be permitted," said Claudia. "Needless to say, it's also forbidden by the Stella Carta. But there are plenty of past examples, and the truth is that every school is willing to resort to such measures if it's deemed necessary."

A faint frown came over Ayato's face. The student council president had just told him that Seidoukan Academy might take similar measures, as well.

"As for the present case, we can probably rule out Gallardworth and Queenvale. They have certain reputations to maintain, and if they were to be exposed doing this, the damage they'd incur is too great. They don't stand to gain enough that way. Now, Le Wolfe excels at this sort of subterfuge, but they're probably concentrating on the Lindvolus. I don't think they would make a move so soon. That leaves us with Jie Long or Allekant... But actually—to be blunt, it doesn't matter."

"It doesn't matter?"

"That's right. The issue at hand is this—if another school is involved, we have to tread carefully, too." Claudia paused and then fixed her gaze on Ayato. "Seidoukan Academy, in fact, has a special military unit under the direct control of the IEF. Even I can't mobilize them without permission from above, but they have far more authority than the disciplinary committee. If I do set them in motion, it won't be long before our enemy finds out. The IEFs monitor each other with the utmost vigilance."

She shrugged in exasperation.

"And when they find out, whichever school is behind these attacks will withdraw. That won't help. We have to obtain proof that another school was involved. Any other outcome is a defeat for us. And our IEF isn't so charitable as to overlook an empty defeat."

"So you can't use this agency unless you have definite proof or a guarantee that you can catch the culprit..."

"Which unfortunately means that they're likely to continue their attacks in the meantime. That's why I wanted to ask a favor of you... Can you be with Julis as much as possible while this is going on?"

"Huh?" At this unexpected request, Ayato stared back at Claudia.

"They will attack her again before long. And I'm afraid that the next time, she may not be able to fend them off alone. I hope you can be there for her when that happens and do what you can. I know this isn't something I should be asking of another student, but..."

"Is there a reason it has to be me?" he asked.

"As you know, she has a tendency to keep others at a distance. But luckily for us, she lets her defenses down with you."

"You think so...? I guess she did show me around campus, but..." It seemed to Ayato that Julis was always angry at him for something.

"You really are slow on the uptake." Claudia giggled.

But Ayato answered seriously. "I understand the situation, but I don't think I can help."

"Oh, why is that?"

"I don't know if a self-assessment has much weight here, but I'm just not that reliable."

"You're too modest."

"It's the truth."

Yes, that's the truth, he thought. *I can't be of much help to Julis just by following her around.*

Claudia gazed questioningly at Ayato for a few moments, then let out a soft sigh. "Well, as I said, just do what you can. Even if that means running away if you feel that you're in danger yourself."

Ayato didn't know what to say.

"Simply having someone nearby could serve as a deterrent, don't you think?"

He sighed. "All right, fine. I'll do it if you insist, but don't expect too much. And this whole thing will be over as soon as you find the one responsible."

"Absolutely," she said with a relieved smile.

"While we're on the subject, can I ask why you're worrying so much about Julis?"

"Oh? Isn't it natural for a student council president to want to protect her fellow students?"

"Is that really all it is?"

Claudia was silent for a bit, averting her gaze, and then she replied quietly, "I came to this school to make my wish come true, just as the other students did. I'm only doing what I must toward that end."

"Your...wish...?" That word stirred a faint twinge of pain for Ayato.

Claudia and Julis—they were both fighting for something. For a wish.

"Oh, I should repay you for agreeing to my favor, shouldn't I?"

"Huh? No, it's fine. You don't have to do anything." Ayato waved in refusal, but she stood up from the bed and slowly drew toward him. "C-Claudia...?"

In response, she only laughed softly, then circled him with her bewitching smile.

Ayato tried to get up, but Claudia snuggled up against to him to restrain him. "Gah!"

"Since we're here, just you and me...," she whispered sweetly at his ear. "You might make a wish that I can grant."

"Wha—!?"

Her hot breath gently caressed his neck, and slowly, she pushed him down against the sofa, until she had half mounted him. The bathrobe had begun to slip from her shoulders, revealing a good portion of her cleavage. In the dimly lit room, her glistening eyes gazed straight into him.

This really can't go any further, Ayato thought, but she was a step beyond scantily clad. He wanted to push her off and had no idea where to put his hands.

"No reason to hold back now…"

"Huh?"

Claudia took Ayato's hand and deliberately placed it against her own chest. "Mm…"

It seemed too soft to be of this world. Her smooth skin seemed to mold to his hand, and that texture was so luscious he thought he would melt simply by touching it. He wanted to be carried away in desire—

"Wait! Stop!" Snapping back to reality in the nick of time, he deftly slid out from under Claudia and in a single motion escaped to the bedroom door. "S-sorry! Well, that's that, I guess! See you!"

He didn't know what was what, but he knew it was too dangerous to stay. Definitely too dangerous.

Claudia was too hard to read, for one thing. He couldn't tell how much of what she did was genuine and how much was just a joke.

If you don't know, then wait until you know. That was what his big sister had told him.

"Oh, what a shame. I did have a feeling that it wouldn't be so easy," he heard Claudia say as he fled the scene.

And he really couldn't be sure what she meant.

✳

"That was close…" Having made his escape from the girls' dormitory, Ayato leaned against the metal fence and let out a breath of relief.

The incredible sensation against his hand from such a short while ago flashed through his mind again and he shook his head vigorously.

"Uh—anyway!" he said to no one in particular and slapped his cheeks.

He didn't have anything against Claudia's request. He cared about Julis, too.

"But…she had the same look as my sister…" Thinking back on it, there was some kind of determination hidden in that gaze. *Then what—*

"Hey!"

"Wha—!?" He snapped to attention at the sudden voice from above. As he looked up in a panic, Julis was leaning out from her windowsill to look down on him.

"What are you doing there?"

"Uh, um, well…" He couldn't exactly tell her that he had just snuck into the girls' dormitory.

"What is it? I can't hear you." Without warning, Julis leaped down from the window.

She was in lounging clothes, very casual. That outfit, along with her actions, made it hard to imagine that she was a princess. "There!"

"Maybe I'm not one to talk, but do you always leave your room that way?"

"Don't be stupid. The other morning when I chased after you was the first time. Although it is rather convenient."

As she approached, Ayato noticed that she held an envelope in her hand. "A letter?"

"Um—yes. Something like that." Julis seemed reluctant to dwell on the subject, but she also looked happy somehow. Maybe it was a letter from someone close to her.

Even in an age when video chat had become prevalent and e-mail was standard, the culture of writing letters hadn't died out. There were myriad reasons why, but one was that there are some things that simply can't be transmitted as data. A less savory reason was that electronic data could be more easily traced.

"So? What are you doing out here at this hour?" said Julis.

"Um… Taking a walk?"

"A walk?"

"Right. I told you I like to walk around." That part wasn't a lie.

"Hmph. Forget it. Are you free on Sunday?"

"The day after tomorrow? Sure, I don't have any plans." He'd just moved here. Of course he didn't have plans.

"Good. Then I can show you around the city like we discussed. I promised, after all."

"Oh, thanks. That'll be really helpful." He remembered that she had told him to leave open one of his days off.

"S-so, about that… Just to be clear, you asked me to be a guide. Isn't that right?"

"Huh? Yeah, I guess so."

"Then, um… This time, I don't want anything to, uh, intrude or throw me off my pace, or…"

Julis seemed unusually inarticulate, but Ayato understood what she wanted to say. "I don't think you need to worry about Saya."

"Why do you think that?"

"She was assigned to make-up class, remember?"

Julis clapped her hands. "Oh, right… Now I remember! Then it's fine. Yes! Good night, then! We'll talk later about how to meet up!" Satisfied, she nodded, then briskly waved her hand and headed back to the dorm, taking the conventional route back to her room.

"The day after tomorrow… I don't think they would try to attack off campus, but I should keep an eye out anyway."

After taking a moment to catch his breath, Ayato, too, headed back to his dorm. His roommate's healthy curiosity might be the death of him if he spent too much time out at this hour.

He looked up to the night sky to see a thin veil of cloud hiding the starlight.

CHAPTER 6
A HOLIDAY FOR TWO

"Hi, Julis. I hope I didn't keep you waiting too…long…"

"No, I just got here myself. I should commend you for being so punctual—hmm? Why is your mouth open like that? You already have a dopey face. Don't make it worse."

It was a clear, bright Sunday. Ayato reached the front gate of the school, where they had agreed to meet up, and found himself frozen at the sight of Julis.

She was wearing a cute black-and-pink dress, rather short, with frilled over-the-knee socks covering her slender legs up to her thighs. Holding a parasol in her hand, she looked *girlish*—a total one-eighty from the image she cultivated at school.

Ayato had known from the beginning that Julis was a beautiful girl, but because she usually carried herself so fiercely, he found himself that much more conscious of her present appearance.

"Do I have something on my face?"

"Oh—uh—sorry! No, it's just that…you look different from usual."

"Wh… I do?"

"Yeah. But you look good."

"Huh? Sh-shut up! Are you *trying* to make me self-conscious?" Julis turned her face away, leaving him with a full view of her blushing cheek. "Th-these are just things I had from home. It's not as if I picked it out special for *you*…"

She was mumbling with a complicated expression, something between embarrassed and annoyed. Then, looking at Ayato again, she said curiously, "You, on the other hand… Maybe there's a better way to put this, but you don't look much better in your own clothes."

"Yeah, I don't have a lot to work with. These are pretty old." Ayato was dressed very casually in a pair of jeans and a three-quarter-sleeve shirt over a T-shirt.

"Well, it's not that you look *bad*, but… Hold on."

"Huh?"

Julis leaned in to put her face close to Ayato's, then started to pat his hair.

"Whoa! Wh-what is it?"

"You're full of cowlicks! I mean, come on. You're not a little kid. You could at least comb your hair before you go outside," Julis scolded, but then giggled at him, her face open and innocent. Meanwhile, Ayato's heart beat faster with every little thing she did.

"All right, let's get going!" Julis led the way in high spirits, whether or not she was aware of his state of mind.

The city of Asterisk was divided into the central district and the outer residential district. A monorail loop line ran through the outer district, connecting the harbor block, the residential area, and the six schools. The main mode of transportation in the central district was a separate subway system. This setup was reportedly intended to prevent duels between students from interfering with public transportation.

Julis and Ayato were in the central district, in front of the main stage of the Festa.

"This is the main stage, the largest stage in Asterisk. All of the championship matches of the Festa take place here," Julis explained, gesturing to the enormous domed structure.

It had a capacity of approximately one hundred thousand. It hosted sellout crowds throughout every Festa tournament. Even now, tourists could be seen here and there taking pictures.

"The design is said to be inspired by the Colosseum of Rome, but it's a different beast altogether," she went on. "There are three other large stages and seven medium-sized stages. And countless smaller outdoor stages."

"Wow, that's a lot."

"Inside the city, you're supposed to use the stages for duels. But... not many people actually do."

"So there are duels in the streets?"

"Yes."

"That has to be pretty dangerous, right?" If Julis were to launch attacks like she had done the other morning, Ayato thought, entire blocks would be scorched.

"People who live here know the risks. So do the tourists—no one enters Asterisk without signing a waiver first. And any damages to stores and residences are compensated."

"So anything goes, huh? I still don't get why everyone wants to come here."

"From a business perspective, having a store in Asterisk is a status symbol and a way to advertise your brand. So they deal with it. There are even some events where the entire central district becomes the stage."

"I wouldn't want to live in a place like this."

"Neither would I," Julis said with a sarcastic smile. "Well? What do you want to do now? Do you want to look around here some more?"

"No, I think I'm set here."

"Hmm. I could take you to the administrative area to see the therapy center. It employs Stregas and Dantes with healing powers, and that's where you end up if you get seriously hurt at the Festa. Although if it's something like a broken bone, they'll send you off for more conventional treatment."

Those with healing abilities were extremely rare, which led to an agreement to gather them in one healing center, so that students of any school could have equal access to care. Because of the limited capacity, however, only patients with life-threatening or debilitating injuries were triaged to the healers.

"Let's see...what else?" Julis mused. "Maybe I should show you the redevelopment area. There's some urban blight that way, bad neighborhoods, but you should know where they are so you don't wander in by accident."

Ayato had heard that the bad neighborhoods were populated with students who were forced to leave the schools for whatever reason and Genestella criminals taking refuge inside the extraterritorial city. It was unsettling, but probably inevitable, that a city with this many people should have a darker side.

"Oh yeah," he said. "Saya told me that she went shopping and got lost in a shady-looking part. She said there were a lot of run-down buildings and shuttered shops."

"That would be the redevelopment area. It would make more sense to go to the commercial area to shop... How did she end up there?"

"Saya has absolutely no sense of direction."

Julis gave him a teasing smirk. "You're one to talk. You have quite a habit of wandering into the strangest places."

Caught out, he flinched. There was no arguing with the truth. Now that she mentioned it, Ayato could recall several occasions when he and Saya had gotten lost together as children.

"So, next up..." Julis opened an air-window to consult a map.

"Hey, Julis? I really appreciate the tour. But do you want to get lunch soon?" Ayato suggested. The hour, as well as his stomach, indicated that it was a good time for lunch.

"Well... I suppose it is about that time..." Julis didn't seem too enthusiastic.

"Is something the matter?"

"No, er, it's just... Lunch sounds fine, but I'm not sure...where to go."

"Aren't there lots of places to eat in the commercial area? Oh, or is everything there superexpensive?" Ayato could imagine that the restaurants there made a business practice of overcharging tourists. But there had to be reasonably priced places as well, considering all the schools.

"No, that's not it. Oh, how do I say this? I'm really sorry!" Julis bobbed her head in apology. "I don't really, um— Actually, I almost never go to the commercial area. So I have no idea where I should take you to eat."

"Oh, okay…"

"I'm such a useless guide… Oh, but I did do some research on the Net! Here!" Julis took out her phone and displayed a list, apparently from a review site.

Ayato's jaw dropped as he looked at it. Everything on the list was a top-notch gourmet restaurant. These were not places that simply gouged tourists. The prices were two digits longer than the ordinary lunch budget. In any case, Ayato doubted that they could sit down in any of these restaurants without a reservation.

"Um, I think those might be a bit much…"

"I—I'm fully aware that these aren't ordinary prices! But these were the only places I had heard of. I wouldn't feel comfortable taking you somewhere I don't know, even if it did have good reviews…"

Indeed, every restaurant on the list was universally renowned—three stars or an equivalent reputation.

"That's okay," Ayato told her with a laugh. "Let's just walk around a bit and see what looks good."

"Is—is that all right?"

"If it's okay with you."

"I'm fine. It's just…you're not upset?" she asked nervously.

"Why would I be?" Ayato said, surprised.

"But…it was so negligent of me."

Julis sounded entirely sincere. *Is there anything she doesn't take so seriously?* he thought.

"I keep wondering, doesn't it make you tired, being so overly conscientious all the time?"

"Well, that's just the way I am, so there's not much I can do about it!" She went sullen, turning away in a huff.

"I'm just worried that you'll get burned out if you keep taking responsibility for everything."

"I like having that kind of weight on my shoulders. That's how I live my life. If you ask me, *you're* the one to worry about. You're like a cloud, floating and impossible to pin down. Why don't you take things more seriously? You'd feel more grounded."

She said the words casually enough, but they stung.

"Uh…" Ayato ham-fistedly changed the subject. "Anyway, should we go over to the commercial area?"

Julis didn't bother to reply aloud. They headed for the most lively part of the commercial area, Main Street.

"Wow, it's packed here."

"Yes. It is the weekend, after all." The neat stone-tiled street overflowed with students—none of them in uniform, but they all wore their school crests, making their status clear. In Asterisk, students were required to wear their crests at all times.

No vehicle traffic was allowed inside the commercial area except at certain hours, so there were only pedestrians to be seen in the street. All sorts of shops were lined up on either side, but the stretch that they were in boasted a high concentration dealing in food and drinks. And the prices advertised on the signs were perfectly reasonable.

"Okay, should we pick something around here?" Ayato turned around to ask Julis—but she wasn't there. "Huh?"

He looked every which way and finally saw her dazzling rose-colored hair a little bit back the way he had come.

"You had me worried. You disappeared all of a sudden," he told her, relieved.

Julis intently turned toward him and asked, "Can we have lunch here?"

"Here…?"

The shop Julis was looking at was a burger franchise. Like the restaurants she had looked up ahead of time, it was also universally well-known, but for an entirely different reason and with entirely different prices.

"It's fine with me…but this is really what you want?" said Ayato.

"Yes! I want to eat here!"

At first he wondered whether she chose this place out of aristocratic curiosity, but from the routine way she ordered and paid, it wasn't a curiosity for her. Ayato asked for a burger and fries with a medium cola—a rather standard order—and the two of them sat down at a patio table.

"This isn't the first time I've asked you this…but are you really a princess?"

"What do you mean?" She even bit into her burger like a regular. But Ayato had to admit that the way she held it in both hands was adorable.

"Well, princesses don't usually eat at fast-food chains, do they?"

"That's a stereotype. You have an actual counterexample sitting in front of you. Accept the facts."

"Well, sure. But…" Ayato leaned back in his seat as he munched on a french fry. It tasted the same as any french fry he'd had since he was little, as any french fry the world over. The constancy of globalization. There was something comforting in that.

"I learned about this place from my friends," Julis said softly after a while, as if recalling a fond memory.

"Friends?"

"I do have some, you know. Well, not here—in my country."

Then, Ayato made the connection. "Oh, the letter you were holding the other day—was that from your friends?"

"*Urk!?*" Julis appeared to choke on her bite of burger. She thumped at her chest as her face turned blue. Hacking, she managed to say, "H-how did you—!?"

"You really are easy to read, Julis."

Now flushing bright red, she turned away from him.

Turning red and blue and red again—what a busy life, Ayato thought.

"Y-you know, this place didn't come up on any of the review sites. Why is that?"

"Well, no one would bother with a place like this."

"Why not? The food is so good," said Julis, genuinely mystified.

Yup, there is something off about her, he thought.

"By the way—can we talk about something serious for a second?" Ayato asked, after she had finished her burger.

"Hmm? What is it?" Julis straightened and looked at him.

"It's about when you were attacked…" Ayato relayed to Julis what Claudia had told him earlier, mostly verbatim. Claudia had not asked him to keep the matter secret, and he thought that having the information would help Julis defend herself.

He left out the part about how he had been asked to help her. He already knew how heartily she would object.

Julis sipped on her cola through a straw as she listened. "Yes, this all sounds plausible. A scheme by another school." She nodded, looking quite unfazed. "I must be their last target. That would explain why they let themselves be seen as they tried to finish me off."

"So, I was thinking maybe you might not want to go out alone or get involved in duels for a while…"

"That's absurd. Why should I have to act differently because of these dirty cowards?"

"…You're right." *I knew she'd say that.*

"I choose my own path. And my will is mine alone."

"Heh. So valiant, as usual." An enormous figure approached from behind her.

"Hello, Lester," she said bitingly without turning around. "Eavesdropping? Such interesting hobbies you have."

Ayato looked up at Lester in surprise. Running into each other on Sunday, off campus and all—for better or worse, Lester and Julis really did seem to have a connection.

"As if I wanted to listen to you," Lester scoffed. "I just happened to hear you talking." Behind him stood the two usual sidekicks. "Heard about you getting attacked by those mystery men. I think you've been pissing off too many people."

"I've done nothing to anger anyone," Julis replied with a straight face.

Lester, in turn, looked astounded. "*That.* You know that attitude is what's getting you so many enemies?"

"No, I don't. I haven't done anything wrong. If that earns enemies, then I'll take them all on."

"Hah. You talk big," said Lester. "Why don't you back up that confidence of yours right now?"

"How many times do I have to say it to get through to that mush you call a brain? I'm not interested in facing you again."

"Just shut up and fight me!" Lester slammed the table so hard that Ayato thought it might snap in two. The patio shook with the noise of the impact, then went silent as conversations ceased.

"L-Lester! You can't force someone to duel in a place like this!"

"He's right, Lester! If you make a scene here, the city guard will be all over us."

Silas and Randy tried desperately to calm him down. Lester didn't seem to hear them.

"Maybe you should back off," said Ayato.

"You keep your mouth shut," Lester replied without looking at him.

"I can't do that. Haven't you heard about how Julis was attacked the other day?"

"So, what's your point?"

"If you pick a fight with Julis here and now, everyone will think you're no different from the ones who attacked her."

That was more than Lester would stand to hear. Now he turned to Ayato to shout at him. "Take that back! You're telling me that *I'm* the same as those sneaking cowards!?" He grabbed Ayato by the collar, dragging him to his feet. "Then maybe I should crush you first."

"Nope. Sorry, but I don't feel like dueling you, either."

"*What?*"

"I have no reason to accept."

Lester shoved Ayato away, his face full of seething rage, then brought his fist down on the table. This time, the unlucky table did split in two. "You call me a coward and then refuse to fight me? You spineless brat!"

"Call me what you want." Ayato coolly shrugged it off.

"Why, you…!"

"Lester, c-calm down! Everyone knows how strong you are! You always fight everyone fair and square. He's so spineless he doesn't know what he's talking about!"

As Lester raised his fist, Randy held him back in a panic. "Th-that's right! You'd never pull a cheap trick like ambushing someone in the middle of a duel—everyone knows that!" Silas anxiously joined in.

Lester growled, glaring at Ayato with barely contained fury. Finally he spun on his heels and wordlessly stalked away.

"Whew..." Ayato brushed at his forehead.

Julis smirked at him. "You really are a tricky one."

"Whatever do you mean?" said Ayato, all innocence.

"Never mind. More importantly..." Her smirk changed to a faint, strained smile and she wiped his lips with a paper napkin. "You had ketchup on your face. I really don't know about you."

*

The sun was sinking when Julis brought the tour to a close.

"Thank you, Julis. I learned a lot, and it was a lot of fun."

"Well... I hate to repeat myself, but I'm only repaying my debt. No need to thank me."

The two walked together through the twilit streets, meandering toward the subway station. Then they noticed some commotion near the entrance.

"Huh? What could that be?"

They approached to find a group of students in a heated argument, about a dozen yelling and jeering at each other. There were curious spectators, too, but most people hurried past, perfectly happy to stay out of it.

"They're from Le Wolfe," Julis muttered. "Behaving like fools, as usual."

The Le Wolfe Black Institute had a reputation for being the most bellicose of the six schools. The culture there valued victory above all else, to the point that school rules and regulations were lax to nonexistent. This resulted in many students who exhibited markedly poor conduct, and the numbers proved it: The majority of dropouts living in the slums were former Le Wolfe students.

"It looks like there are two sides arguing...," said Ayato. "Ooh, it just got physical."

A student who looked like the leader of one of the groups shoved another student, prompting both sides to draw their weapons. In the blink of an eye, the altercation had escalated to a brawl.

"This is bad. We've been set up."

"Huh?" Just as Ayato was about to ask Julis what she meant, a student holding a Lux knife lunged at them.

"Whoa!" Ayato managed to evade with a light step—but it had clearly been meant for him. The attacker was already disappearing amid the skirmish.

Meanwhile, Ayato and Julis suddenly found themselves surrounded by fighting Le Wolfe students.

"This is a trick that those idiots at Le Wolfe use to attack someone in the streets. They surround the target during a brawl and rough them up, and then simply pretend that the target got mixed up by chance. I had heard about it, but this is the first time I've gotten pulled in," Julis explained while repelling several attackers.

So that argument they were having was all an act. Ayato looked around and saw that the students clashing swords seemed to be just going through the motions. They intermittently threw sharp glances toward himself and Julis as if looking for a chance to attack. "They sure go through a lot of trouble…"

"Both sides probably went through the procedure for proper duels," said Julis. "They'll have a defense even if they get rounded up by the city guard."

They would still be punished in that case, but apparently, the administration was often forgiving where duels were involved.

"Does this mean that the people after you are from Le Wolfe?" Ayato asked.

"Not necessarily. Goons like these will do almost anything for a little cash. Oop!" As she dodged a Lux arrow, Julis smiled mischievously. "Besides, they're all weaklings."

"Uh…so what should we do?" Ayato could guess what she would say but asked anyway.

"Do I need to tell you? This is obviously a self-defense situation. So we'll crush them and squeeze some answers out of them."

"I'm not sure that's the best idea…" The brawl itself was probably a trick to get Julis's guard down. There could be another sniper aiming as they spoke.

"Don't worry. I can roast them whole and still look out for an ambush." Flames rose up around Julis.

"Maybe you could let them off with just medium rare?" Ayato halfheartedly suggested.

*

The Le Wolfe students turned out to be poor fighters. The vast majority of them lay on the ground, plumes of smoke rising.

A few of them had tried to run, and from their shouts of dismay ("That's the Glühen Rose!" "This wasn't part of the deal!"), it was clear that they hadn't even known who they were attacking.

"Hmph. Hardly even a warm-up." Julis combed her fingers through her hair and ignored the heaps of bodies to glare viciously at Ayato. "But you—what was that all about?"

"Wh-what was what now?"

"What was that pathetic fight you put up!? That was really all you could do against *them*!?"

Julis had reason to be angry. She was the one who had defeated most of the goons, while it was all Ayato could do to evade the relentless attacks flying at him from every direction. Even if none of them were particularly skilled, they presented enough problems as a group surrounding him.

"Well, yeah. As I am now, that's the best I can do."

Julis stared at him dubiously and finally let out a long sigh. "Apparently, I overestimated you."

The disappointment in her voice was unmistakable. Ayato could only smile apologetically.

"Forget it. Right now, we need to get some answers out of them."

Julis examined several of the Le Wolfe students on the ground, then yanked up one with a Mohawk. Ayato remembered that he was the leader of one of the squabbling groups.

"You. How long are you going to pretend to be unconscious? Wake up. Or I'll torch this freakish haircut of yours right to the scalp." The threat worked splendidly, as the student with the Mohawk snapped his eyes open with a frightened yelp.

"I want nice, clear answers. Who hired you?"

"I—I don't know anything! We just got told to rough you guys up a little! He didn't even say why!"

"What did he look like?"

"A huge, tall dude wearing all black. I didn't see his face!"

"Did you recognize his voice?"

"His v-voice? No, I dunno."

"You mean it was a voice you didn't know?"

"No, the dude didn't say a word. The job was written out on a piece of paper that was with the cash."

"A piece of paper…? What else did it say?"

"That this was an advance and they'd pay the rest after they confirmed the job was done."

"Confirm…" As Julis seemed lost in thought, the student with the Mohawk suddenly opened his eyes wide.

"H-him! It was him! He hired us to do this!"

Just as Ayato and Julis turned to look, the shadow fled into the alleys. They only caught a glimpse, but there was no mistake—it was a large male clad in black.

"Stop!" Julis ran after the shadow.

"Julis, don't! It might be a trap!" Ayato called.

She turned to glance back at him, but did not give up her pursuit. She must be furious to act so recklessly. Which was precisely the opening her attackers were hoping for.

"What—!?" The large figure had been waiting for Julis in the alley and now swung his enormous battle-ax at her.

Julis leaped aside to dodge the blow, only to be attacked by another man clad in black. This one held a Lux assault rifle. As bullets of light rained down on her, she evaded the barrage by rolling on the ground. Her reflexes were nothing short of astonishing.

I can make it!

Just as Ayato was about to jump in between Julis and the second attacker, a shadow on a rooftop caught the corner of his eye. One more black-clad man stood atop the building, aiming a Lux crossbow.

A third one—!

The target of the next attack was not Julis, but Ayato. The arrow of light sliced through the wind toward Ayato. A perfectly timed sniper shot.

Deciding that he couldn't dodge it, he made a quicker move and drew his Lux activator to use as a shield. The exterior shattered, fragments piercing his clothes. Luckily for him, the core stopped the arrow, but the activator was probably unusable now.

As he breathed a sigh of relief, Ayato marveled at the attackers' skill in finding just the right instant to strike. These people must be of stunningly bad character.

"Hey! Are you all right!?" Julis ran to him, looking quite stern.

"Barely. My clothes are ruined, though." Ayato smiled wryly at her and looked around to find that the attackers were already gone. They were also experts at fleeing the scene of the crime.

The Le Wolfe students who had been sprawled on the ground until moments ago were also scattering in clusters.

"The city guard will be here any second now," said Julis. We should get out of here, too."

"Are you sure?"

"We've done nothing they could hold us for, but I don't want to have to explain everything, either. Besides, we finally have a clue. I'm not about to let the cops have all the fun with it." Her eyes burned with rage as she spoke. "This is too much. I won't be satisfied unless I settle the score with my own hands."

"You're their target. Maybe...you could be a little careful?"

Julis replied with a "hmph," and Ayato wondered if he should take that for acquiescence.

In any case, he probably had to report this to Claudia...

"By the way, are you free after this?" she said.

"Huh? I guess I don't have any plans..."

In the settling dusk, Julis stared at Ayato at length as if to inspect him. "Then come to my room."

"Huh…?"

*

Still, he couldn't exactly stride into the girls' dormitory through the front gate.

"Hi, it's me… Man, I really hate how I'm getting used to this." Once again, here he was coming into Julis's room through the window.

Even if he hadn't known it the first time, this was Ayato's third time coming into the dorm this way. It sent a shiver down his spine to think what the dormitory watch might do to him if they found out.

"Oh, you're here. Sorry, just give me a few more seconds." Julis, having gone home ahead of him, was rummaging for something in a corner.

Ayato sat down on the windowsill and looked around the room, noting its considerable size. It must have been a perk of being a Page One, like Claudia's room was.

The atmosphere of Julis's room, however, was markedly different. What stood out here was the number of plants. With rows of pots and planters, it looked like a small botanical garden, but carefully arranged so that one could still walk around the room unimpeded. Some of the plants were flowering beautifully, and just looking at them was calming.

"The last time I was here, I didn't really get to take in the surroundings," Ayato thought aloud. And if he tried to remember, too many of the images that came up were supple and fair… The way she'd looked that morning…

"There, I found it."

"*Augh!* S-sorry!"

"Why are you apologizing?" Julis tilted her head at him.

"Oh, uh, nothing… So why did you want me here?" He wasn't

necessarily trying to change the subject—or so he tried to tell himself. It was a legitimate question.

There was still some time until lights-out, but the sun was long gone from the sky. Just like with Claudia the other night, Ayato found that being invited to a girl's room at this hour was something of a strain on his mental health.

"Right. Let's get this over with. Take off your clothes."

"Wha—!?" Ayato flailed backward and almost fell from the window. "Um, uh—J-ju-ju-Julis?"

"Why are you so upset? Just hurry up and—" In the middle of her sentence, Julis realized the reason for his consternation, and her face steadily flushed into bright red. "Y-you idiot! Wh-wh-what did you think I meant? I'm only offering to mend your ripped clothes!"

"Clothes…?" Ayato remembered that his clothes were torn from that attack outside the subway station. "Oh—mend them? You can sew, Julis?"

"I'm not the best there is, but I can manage," she replied sullenly. "I bear some responsibility for what happened. I don't want to incur any more debts to you."

"Well, if you're offering…okay." Ayato obediently removed his shirt and handed it to her.

Julis threaded the needle from her sewing set and began to stab it through the fabric with unsteady hands. She did seem a little clumsy, but she wasn't a complete novice, either.

"Let me guess… Did you learn that from your friends, too?"

"Good guess." Julis nodded without looking up as she concentrated on the needle.

"I had a feeling." Ayato watched her sew for a while, then resumed looking around the room anew once he saw that he was worrying too much about her.

Unlike Claudia's place, Julis's was a studio, but that single room was larger than either of Claudia's rooms, tidily kept and neatly organized. Next to the bed was a sturdy desk, with a rose in a small vase on the corner, and beside that a photograph—a rarity these days.

Curious, Ayato went for a closer look. It showed a woman who looked like a nun with children of varying ages. Judging from their appearance, they did not seem very well-off.

There was one child, however, who stood out from the others. She was dressed just as plainly as the rest of the children, but even from a photograph, the difference in upbringing was clear. She looked carefree, smiling just as happily as the other children—with her dazzling rose-colored hair.

"Hey, Julis. Are…these kids your friends?"

"Hmm…? Hey! Did I say you could go through my things!?" Julis rushed toward him, flustered, and snatched the picture from his hand.

"The girl in the middle… That's you, right?"

Julis shot him a piercing glare, then let out a sigh and placed the photograph back on the desk.

"Yes. You're right, this is a picture of my friends," she said, then returned to her seat to finish sewing. "It might be hard to imagine, but I was a tomboy growing up…"

"Hard to imagine?" *Wait, a tomboy growing up? Then, what is she now?*

"You have something to say?"

"Not at all. Please continue."

"Hmph. Anyway, I would often sneak out of the palace as a child. It was too stifling, I guess. My family has royal blood, but not a direct line of descent. When the monarchy was reestablished, there were very few bloodlines left and our family was chosen for the throne." Her needle never paused as she went on. "But one day, I went farther than usual and I got lost. I wandered for some time and eventually ended up in a bad part of town. Lieseltania is a relatively safe country, but you can imagine what might happen to an affluent-looking child drifting by herself in a place like that."

"How developed were your powers then?" Ayato asked.

"Enough to make a little flame like a lighter. Not very useful. And even with more of my power, I still would have been helpless, never having been in a fight before. A mean bunch spotted me and herded me into an alley. I couldn't do anything—I was just crying. Then, just in time, *they* came and saved me. Can you imagine how I felt? Those girls were heroes to me." She spoke with a fierce admiration that clearly hadn't dimmed since that day.

"After I made my way back to the palace, I found out that they lived in an orphanage in the slums. And I would keep sneaking out of the palace to follow them around. They saw me as a nuisance at first, but I was so stubborn that somehow we ended up becoming friends." Now her voice was shaded with fond reminiscence.

"Did those girls know you were a princess?"

"No, I hid it from them at the time. But the nuns must have known."

"What about your family?"

"Everyone around me tried like mad to stop me. But by that time, my father and mother were already dead, and I didn't care what the others said."

"Wha…?" Ayato faltered.

"Hmm? Oh, you didn't know. The current king of Lieseltania is my brother. The previous rulers were my parents. But I don't remember them very well."

"I… I didn't know…" Ayato could hardly remember his mother, either, and he knew firsthand that there was nothing much anyone else could say about those things.

"What surprised me when I looked it up was that their orphanage was built by a charitable foundation that my mother started. So I couldn't help but feel a connection." With that, Julis's hands suddenly fell idle. "But that charity no longer exists. There are more orphans every year, and it's only getting harder to keep the orphanage running. That's why I came here. This time, I have to save them—I have to protect them. It's sad, but the thing that those children need the most right now is money."

"But wait…"

"Let me stop you right there. No one asked me to do this. I'm doing it out of my own free will and for myself. I'm only doing the thing I want to do at this moment," Julis declared with her forthright gaze.

Ayato believed it wholeheartedly. *This was all her idea, hers alone. That's the sort of person she is.*

But that wasn't the question on his mind. "No, I mean… Aren't there plenty of other ways?"

"Ways for what?"

"You know…to do something about the money. Aren't you the princess, after all?"

Julis shrugged her shoulders and scoffed. "As if the country has any money for me to spend. The allowances for the royal family are drawn from a budget voted on by the parliament. Lieseltania is nothing but a puppet of the IEFs. You think they'd allow a social welfare project without outlook for a penny of profit? That's why my mother's foundation was shut down in the first place. And my country's people never raised a word of protest."

The integrated enterprise foundations put economic activity above all else, and they did not hesitate to alter the very ethical fabric of society to suit their goals. Over time, they would massage public opinion and gradually change culture in their favor. Ayato was now standing in the concrete embodiment of that effort—the city of Asterisk.

"There is money to spend *on* me, but none that I can spend. So, the only thing I can do is to earn it. Luckily for me, I have the talents of a Strega. And the title of a princess must have worked in my favor when I applied. What an ideal marketing package I make." She made a low, bitter laugh. "This worthless, despicable city. They have students fight each other and the world goes mad over it. Greed swirls in this place, swallowing up everything and fattening itself. It's hideous and it only keeps getting bigger. But that's exactly why this city lies closest to every possible desire. This is where I will make my wish come true. That's my reason to fight."

Julis spread out Ayato's shirt with a snap. It was…well, it was repaired enough to be functional, even if the result was not particularly attractive.

"There!" she announced. "Now take this and go home."

"Okay. Thanks."

"We owe each other nothing now."

"Yes, I know."

Not a good place to overstay my welcome, Ayato thought—and then noticed a neatly folded handkerchief on the corner of the table. That little handkerchief had been the catalyst for their meeting. But now he was getting an inkling of its significance.

Julis noticed what he was looking at and smiled, gently picking it up. "The girls from the orphanage gave this to me for my birthday. Everyone helped embroider it. The stitches that look the worst are by my best friend."

That person must be really important to her, he thought.

"It's my greatest treasure," she said with a shy smile, then set the handkerchief back down.

The sight stirred a warmth in Ayato's chest—and at the same time a dull pain.

Someone important. Something to protect.

…The thing that I have to do.

"Well, see you tomorrow." He pulled his shirt on, waved good-bye, and leaped down from the window.

The whisper of a thought darted through his mind. *So that's a reason to fight…*

CHAPTER 7
UNCHAINED

"What's up, Amagiri? You're spacing out."

Eishirou's voice startled him, even though they were walking side by side.

"Oh, um, nothing. It's nothing." Ayato waved the question away and hurriedly forced a smile.

"Huh... Well, if you say so. But you've been acting kinda funny since yesterday."

"I'm fine. I just didn't get enough sleep... Um, anyway, we better hurry, or we'll be late."

"Don't sweat it. We'll slide into homeroom just in time." So Eishirou said, but the halls were already almost deserted. In fact, the two arrived at their classroom a few seconds before homeroom began.

"I can't believe you went back to sleep after I woke you up, Yabuki... We barely made it."

"Aw, let it go. We're on time, aren't we?"

"It's the principle of the— Oh, hey. Morning, Julis."

As Ayato took his seat, Julis at her neighboring desk was intently scanning a letter. She made no reply.

"Julis?"

"Uh— Oh, hi." Julis put away the letter in a rush and averted her eyes from his.

"Yo! Butts in seats now! I'm takin' attendance!" Kyouko stormed into the room looking downright bloodthirsty, and Ayato had no chance to pursue his curiosity about Julis's behavior.

She also seemed distracted in class, her mind obviously elsewhere.

Ayato approached her after school, when he thought they could finally talk. "Julis, is something wrong?"

She got up from her seat without even looking at him. "Sorry. I have plans today."

"Huh? H-hey, Julis?" Ayato could only look on as Julis swiftly left the classroom, deaf to him.

"I wonder what's wrong...?"

"Uh-oh. Looks like she's back to her old self," Eishirou supplied.

"Her old self?"

Eishirou shrugged. "Her Highness was always like that before you came along. She had this 'leave me alone' vibe. And just when I thought she was beginning to thaw! What a shame."

Ayato was worried about Julis, but he had to report to Claudia about yesterday's incident. Anyway, if something else was bothering Julis, maybe Claudia would know...

"Oh, good day. What can I do for you?"

Ayato entered the student council room, and Claudia greeted him with her usual smile.

"We had some trouble again yesterday."

"Yes, I did hear about that. They used Le Wolfe students."

"News reaches you fast." That wasn't what he wanted to talk about, though. "So, I might have an idea of who's behind the attacks."

Even Claudia couldn't hide her surprise at this. "Really?"

"Yes, I'm mostly certain."

As he murmured his reasoning to her, Claudia sat deep in thought.

"I see... All right. I'll investigate on my end, too. I hope this will put an end to the matter..." But Claudia seemed somewhat dissatisfied.

"Is something bothering you?"

"Does Julis know about this, too?"

"We didn't talk about it, but I think she could have figured it out on her own."

"And where is she now?"

"She went home in a hurry saying she had plans… Oh no—!" Now Ayato understood.

Of course. With Julis being the way she is, if she realized who was behind the attacks, there's no way she would leave the rest to someone else.

"This could be just a little bad," said Claudia.

"But would she really confront them face-to-face? Without hard evidence, they'll just deny everything…"

"No, at this point, they probably wouldn't drag it out any longer. They would move to silence her with everything they have. They may even contact her first and—"

"That letter this morning!" Ayato blurted.

"Letter?"

"This morning in homeroom—Julis was looking at a letter. I thought it was strange because she tried to hide it."

Claudia paled. "In any case, then we should find her immediately."

"But where do we look?"

For all that it was an artificial island, Asterisk was not small. They had little chance of finding Julis by searching aimlessly.

"First, I'll check to see if she returned to her dorm after class," said Claudia. "If our enemy suggested a meeting, they would choose somewhere deserted. That helps narrow our search."

She displayed a map of Asterisk in an air-window.

"Oh, hold on…" Someone was calling Ayato on his mobile. He opened the air-window in a hurry, thinking that it could be Julis.

"*…Ayato, help me.*"

The girl who appeared in the window was Saya, her brows drawn with worry.

"Saya? What's the matter?"

"*I'm lost.*"

Ayato pressed his hand against his forehead in disbelief at her answer.

"Again, Saya? …I can't help, though, sorry. We're busy with Julis right now—"

"*Riessfeld? I thought I just saw her…*"

Ayato and Claudia exchanged glances.

"Really?"

In her tiny video-chat image, Saya nodded.

"Saya! Tell me exactly where you saw her! No, wait—where are you, anyway?"

"...*If I knew, I wouldn't be lost.*"

When she's right, she's right, Ayato thought.

"Pardon me," Claudia interrupted. "Miss Sasamiya, can you let us see your surroundings?"

"*Like this?*" Saya seemed a bit confused by the sudden third-party request, but she readily obliged.

"You're outside the redevelopment area. I think I can narrow down your whereabouts."

Ayato was impressed that it took Claudia only one look to know where she was.

"Thanks, Saya! You're a huge help!"

"*...I still need help.*"

"Oh, right. Umm..." For a moment, he considered asking Saya to join the rescue operation, but then thought it might be too dangerous to involve her if their enemy was about to let loose this time. And even if he told Saya where to go, she probably wouldn't be able to get there on her own.

"I'll send someone to pick up Miss Sasamiya," said Claudia. "Ayato, you'll find Julis."

"Thanks, Claudia."

"Oh, no trouble at all," she replied brightly and then highlighted the possible locations on the map one after another. Her work went remarkably quickly, but Ayato still found his patience tried, a symptom of the situation's urgency.

"I wonder why Julis didn't say anything, though," he complained. He knew she wanted to take care of it herself, and yet... "Maybe she still doesn't trust me."

"I think it's the opposite," said Claudia, giving him a wry smile without taking her eyes off the map.

"What do you mean?"

"I told you before, remember? She's doing all she can to protect what she has. And you can probably count yourself as 'someone important to her."

"Julis? Protect...me?"

In that moment, something burst open inside him. A new vista spread out before his eyes.

"Oh..." He remembered his sister's words from that night. She'd told him that she would protect him. And he told her that he would protect her. He'd failed to keep that promise, but... "It really is that simple."

Now he understood. *I know what it is that I have to do.*

"All done!" Claudia sent the map to his mobile.

"Okay. I'm off!" he said, already thinking of how he'd check each place, starting with the closest.

"Oh, just one moment. Before you go—" Claudia called him back as he was about to fly out of the room like a shot. "It's ready. You're free to take it with you."

*

Julis went to an abandoned building in the redevelopment area.

Twilight gloom reigned over the partially demolished edifice. Fragmentary walls and floors created an illusion of open space, but the piles of debris made for numerous blind spots.

Undaunted, she walked farther into the building. Her face was grim as she stepped steadily onward through the uncanny shadows projected by the lowering sun.

As soon as she had set foot into the back of the plot, debris fell from an upper story whose floor no longer existed—falling right toward where she stood. It was more than enough material to crush a girl.

"Burst into bloom...," she murmured, without even looking up. *"Red Crown."*

A five-sided flower materialized to shield her, like an umbrella made of flame, and repelled every piece of the falling debris.

"You must know by now that it'll take more than that to beat me? Show yourself already, Silas Norman."

The moon floated dimly beyond the gaping holes in the structure. Steel reinforcement bars crashed into the floor and a lone boy emerged from the clouds of dust.

"My apologies. That didn't even make for a good pregame show." The thin boy, Silas, bowed theatrically. "I'm impressed. How did you know that I was behind those attacks?"

"A slip of the tongue yesterday."

"Yesterday?" Silas cocked his head. "Hmm. How *did* I slip up?"

Julis answered him with forced composure. "Yesterday, in the commercial area, when Ayato got Lester riled up. When you tried to restrain him, you said that he would never ambush someone in the middle of a duel."

"…So what?"

"How do you know that the attackers ambushed me in the middle of a duel? The first attack during my duel with Ayato didn't make the news."

"But the second attack did. I saw it myself."

"Yes, that one did. But all the outlets reported only that I repelled the attackers. No one mentioned Sasamiya, or even the fact that another student was at the scene. What a farce, when she was the one who fought you off."

Silas stared inscrutably back at her.

"Do you understand yet? To talk about a duel, when it wasn't even publicized that someone else was there, you would have to have been there or have heard about it from someone who was. Either possibility points to you being the attacker or an accomplice."

"My, my…how careless of me. So he provoked Lester on purpose."

"Probably. I wouldn't put that sort of subterfuge past him," Julis said, beaming with a hint of pride.

"Hmm. Then I was right to redirect my attention to him. He's too great of an obstacle if I want to get to you."

"Why, you—!"

Silas laughed. "I know, I know! That's the entire reason you came all the way out here—to stop me from doing just that."

Watching him spread his arms with a cocky smirk, Julis ground her teeth.

That morning, she had found a letter in her desk reading: *"I will now target those close to you. If you don't want that to happen, come to the address below."*

"Then let's get this over with."

"Please, no need to be so hasty! I'd love nothing more than to talk this out like adults. That's why I asked you here in the first place."

"A bald-faced lie if I ever heard one. You expect me to believe you?"

"Oh, but I'm serious. To be perfectly frank, I'd rather avoid facing you in a real battle if I can." Even as Silas admitted this, he was no less self-assured.

Julis had done her homework before coming here. Silas was unranked, and he had no records from official matches. As far as fighting went, he was a complete unknown.

Besides, there were at least three attackers. Even if Silas was one of them, that meant he had two accomplices.

"Very well. I'll hear you out." It would be better to wait and see how Silas wanted to play this, Julis decided.

"Wonderful. The truth is, I'm here for the money—just like you. I thought we could understand one another." Silas nodded, smiling broadly. "You might have already guessed, but what I want is for you to withdraw from the Phoenix. And if you could also state for the record that I had nothing to do with these attacks, that would be a nice plus."

"And what's in it for me?"

"Your and Ayato Amagiri's well-being. Is that insufficient?"

"It's ridiculous," Julis said flatly. "I can have that if I crush you here. And even if I were to keep my mouth shut, the student council is already onto you, I'm sure."

"I'm not worried about them. There isn't a shred of evidence that I was involved."

"You seem awfully sure of that."

"Because it's the truth."

They glared squarely at each other.

Then a furious voice rumbled through the broken building. "Just what the hell is going on here, Silas!?"

"—Lester?" Julis started at the sight of Lester MacPhail stomping onto the scene. She had fallen into her fighting stance before she understood that his anger was directed at Silas.

"Hello, Lester. I've been waiting for you."

"You said Julis agreed to duel me, so I rushed over here, but this... Is this true? *You're* the one who attacked Julis?" He had clearly heard everything.

"Yes, that's right. You have a problem with that?"

"Don't be an idiot! Why the hell would you do that!?"

"Why? I can only tell you that I was asked to."

"Asked to...?" The look on Lester's face was a mishmash of surprise, anger, and confusion.

If that was an act, it would take some considerable thespian talent. Julis knew perfectly well that Lester had no such ability.

She let out a sigh and said, "He was working with another school to attack the favorites for the Phoenix. So, you didn't know?"

Lester was speechless, his face frozen in shock. Silas, on the other hand, must have played a convincing part as the obedient sidekick.

Silas gave Lester a mocking look and shrugged his shoulders. "Unlike the two of you, I'd rather avoid foolishness like fighting face-to-face over and over again. If there's a safer and more efficient way to make my money, it's only natural to take it."

"That's why you sold out your fellow students?" said Julis.

"*Fellow* students? You must be joking." Silas laughed, shaking his head. "Every single person gathered here is an enemy to every other, you see. We might make temporary alliances for team competitions or tag matches, but aside from that, we're all out to get ahead at the expense of anyone else. I'd think that you two of all people would understand that, with your high rankings. You fight with everything you have, paying for your status with sweat and blood, gaining your place only to be hounded by those who would take it out from under you. I'm not interested in such a troublesome life. If I can make just as much money without standing out, that's obviously the wise choice—wouldn't you agree?"

"Well, I do see the point you're trying to make. It is true that the students here aren't out to make friends with each other. And it's true that the more famous you get, the more troublesome people come for you."

"Hey...Julis!" Lester scowled, keenly aware of having been called out.

"But that's *not* all there is."

"No? How disappointing. I always thought that you and I were of a similar mind."

"*You're* disappointed? To think I'd have anything in common with a lowlife like you." Julis glared at Silas, signaling she had nothing left to say to him.

"I'll ask you before I pummel you into the ground," Lester spoke up. "Why did you call me here? If you actually thought I'd take your side, you're much stupider than you look."

"No, you're more like insurance. I needed someone to play the role of the guilty attacker, in case the negotiations with Miss Riessfeld here fell through."

"Are you actually an idiot? Why would I agree to that?"

"Oh, no need to worry. When the two of you can't speak, I can write whatever script I want to fit my needs. Well, I suppose the easiest thing would be to say that you dueled so fiercely that it resulted in a deadly draw."

At that, Lester's fuse blew completely. "That's a laugh. You think you can shut me up with your puny powers? Let's see you try." He drew his Lux activator, and the weapon that took shape was an enormous battle-ax as large as his frame—the Bardiche-Leo.

"Lester, don't rush into combat. We don't know what he has up his sleeve. Isn't he a Dante?" Julis hardly thought of Lester as a trusted friend, but she wasn't about to abandon him in a situation like this.

"Yeah, his power is telekinesis," Lester scoffed. "It's probably all he can do to toss around some rubble. Anyway, Julis—*you* stay out of this!"

Before he'd even finished the sentence, he launched at Silas and swung his crescent-shaped ax, its blade of light howling through the air. "Go to hell! What the—!?"

At that instant, a giant clad in black fell from the hole in the ceiling to insert himself between Lester and his opponent and stopped his attack—with its bare hands.

He growled as he strained to push his ax forward, channeling all his might into it, but the giant did not budge an inch. Lester, who had thought himself the most physically formidable student at Seidoukan, was stunned.

Even as he stared in surprise, he had enough presence of mind to jump back.

"Oh, I get it," he spat. "So *this* is your friend."

"Friend?" Silas gave a condescending chuckle. "Don't be silly." He snapped his fingers, and two more men clad in black appeared from the shadows. "These are my cute, adorable dolls."

The men shed their black robes, revealing themselves to be just that—dolls. Their faces had indentations that suggested eyes, but no noses or mouths. In fact they were mostly featureless. They bore a slight resemblance to ball-jointed mannequins, only far more eerie.

"Battle Puppets...?" Julis observed calmly.

Remote-controlled Puppets could be used in combat but required dedicated facilities for operation. Julis found it unlikely in the extreme that Silas could build such a large-scale infrastructure. Not impossible per se, but to do so in Asterisk while managing to keep it a secret would be as close to impossible as one could get.

"I'd rather you didn't compare them to such unrefined toys," said Silas. "My beauties have no machinery whatsoever."

Then how can they move? But right before their eyes, the dolls moved as smoothly as people.

"So, *this* is your power." Julis finally understood why she could never sense the presence of the attackers until the very last moment. It was simply because they were inorganic. They *had* no presence, no fighting spirit there for her to sense.

"All this time, you were hiding it from me!?" Lester shouted. "You said that it was the best you could do to manipulate a knife."

"You actually believed that!?" Silas burst into laughter. "Oh, forgive me. But think about it. What kind of fool tips his hand to his enemies?"

He shrugged grandly and went on. "As Lester just mentioned, my ability entails using mana to control objects that I've marked. So long as it's inorganic, I can manipulate it as I please—even complex structures like these dolls. Of course, no one at our school knows this."

Julis saw some of the reason why Silas was so self-assured. "You used the dolls to attack your targets. If no one knows about your ability, then it certainly would be hard to catch you."

Ayato had said that Silas had the perfect alibi. It would be easy to establish with this ability. Whatever the range of his remote-control powers might be, there was no need for him to be at the scene if he could see what was going on. All he had to do was equip one of the dolls with a camera.

The reality was that it was difficult to prove Stregas and Dantes guilty of wrongdoing when they abused their powers like this—which was exactly why every nation required those so gifted to register.

"Enough with this!" said Lester. "I'll knock you down and hand you over to the disciplinary committee or the city guard, and that'll be it for you!"

"That's assuming you can leave here unharmed," Silas replied smugly.

"You asked for it…!" As Lester raised his prana, the blade of the Bardiche-Leo almost doubled in size.

Julis had seen this several times in the past. It was Lester's deadly Meteor Arts move. His weapon now resembled a giant hammer rather than an ax.

"Take this! *Blast Nemea!*"

With a tearing shout, Lester swung, sending the three dolls flying. They smashed spectacularly into a pillar, pieces scattering, and the pillar cracked from the force.

Two of the dolls were completely destroyed, limbs broken off and bodies twisted into impossible positions. But the giant doll had suffered no more than a fracture in the torso. It wrenched itself from the pillar and faced Lester as if the blow had been a slight breeze.

"Hah, this one's pretty sturdy." Lester grinned, having no shortage of confidence himself.

"This is a heavyweight model that I built to face you," said Silas. "Much more durable than the normal model. Its body type and weapon were also designed with you in mind. I need it to play your part when the need arises."

"To frame me, huh? Then that one over there with the crossbow is supposed to be Randy?"

"That's about the size of it."

"Lot of work you put in," Lester remarked. "Too bad it's all going to waste!"

He swung down the Bardiche-Leo again—but just as the blade was about to make contact with the heavyweight doll, two new dolls emerged from behind a pillar and peppered him with bullets of light. He roared in pain.

"Lester!" Julis tried to come to his aid, but yet another doll appeared to block her path.

"I need you to stay right there, if you would," Silas told her. "Oh yes—those ones are also specially equipped. They have increased heat resistance to withstand you."

Three more dolls surrounded Julis. Unlike the others, their bodies were jet-black, but otherwise they looked the same. And they held Lux swords in their hands.

Julis activated her own Lux, the Aspera Spina.

"Can't you do anything besides cheap ambushes...?" Lester heaved himself up to one knee, clearly in pain, and glared at Silas.

"Oh, look at that. I didn't think you'd be getting up again!"

Lester must have diverted all his prana to defense. He was bleeding here and there, but his will to fight seemed unabated.

Everyone had a limited supply of prana. If it was depleted, the fighter would lose consciousness—and doing so in these circumstances would mean much worse for Lester.

"Go ahead, throw as many of these blockheads at me as you can. They're no match for—"

"Oh, poor Lester... You really don't understand a thing."

As Silas spoke, another doll jumped down in front of Lester—followed by another and another.

Lester looked on furiously, but his expression transformed

gradually into incredulity and then fear. Julis, trying to get past the dolls surrounding her, stopped in her tracks, wide-eyed.

They were not looking at ten dolls or even twenty. There were far more than that...

"Throw as many of them at you as I can? Very well, I'll do exactly as you wish. The maximum number of dolls I can control at one time is one hundred and twenty-eight."

"A hundred and..." Despair spread over Lester's face.

Looking down on him, Silas hummed with pleasure. "Oh, what a nice expression. That's just the kind of face I hoped you would make. Well, then—nice knowing you!"

He waved his arm once and the dolls descended on Lester.

"Silas, don't!" Julis tried to break through the wall of dolls surrounding her, but against their numbers, there was nothing she could do. While the things were not that strong individually, they fought effectively as a team.

Silas looked at Julis with a thin smile on his face. From behind him, she could hear Lester's muffled screams—but before long, they stopped.

"Don't worry. I still need him alive," Silas prattled. "I have to make it look like you finished him off. I'll just need to find something flammable and—"

"Burst into bloom—*Antirrhimum Majus!*"

Julis didn't have the patience to let Silas finish his monologue. She waved her sword and a magic circle took form along the arc of its path. With a fierce blast of heat, an enormous dragon made of flame tore forth from the circle.

"Ah. This I haven't seen before," Silas murmured, impressed.

He certainly shouldn't have seen it before, Julis thought. This move was her trump card. She did not show it off needlessly.

The dragon of fire shook the air with a powerful roar, then crushed the dolls that were blocking the way with a single bite of its mighty jaw.

Silas exclaimed in surprise to see his dolls, including the models

with increased heat resistance, helplessly destroyed by such awesome destructive power.

"Now, that is quite something. I suppose there's a reason you're ranked fifth…" He backed away and snapped his fingers again. "But I still have you outnumbered!"

Five dolls made their way past the dragon's maw to surround Julis and attack. Gritting her teeth, she fought back with the Aspera Spina, but controlling the dragon took a good part of her concentration, and her movements were dulled. As she barely blocked a blade of light with her own, the interference of Lux weapon contact threw off dazzling sparks.

"I'm not done yet!" With a yell, Julis kicked the doll in the midsection to send it flying, then whirled to push away the weapon of the doll behind her and plunged her sword into that one.

But the doll continued indifferently and wrapped its arms around her. "What—it sacrificed itself!?"

Silas laughed. "If you fight them as if they're human, they'll take advantage of you like that." Several dolls, lined up in a row, readied their guns in unison.

Julis called back her dragon to shield her from the barrage, but not in time. Bullets of light ripped through the dancing flames and into her thigh.

As she bit down on a cry and fell to her knees, two dolls grabbed her by either arm and pressed her against a wall. The fire dragon melted away into thin air.

"Your spells are powerful, but they also blind you from incoming attacks," said Silas.

"Heh. You're pretty observant," Julis replied, forcing her grimace of pain into a challenging grin. "But I figured out something, too."

"Oh? What would that be?"

"It's Allekant that's backing you." She watched the smile vanish from his face. "You said those dolls were specially made. Where did you get armor strong enough to withstand my attacks and Lester's? And enough to mass-produce them in those numbers? No other school has the technological capacity."

"Very insightul. But now I definitely can't let you walk away from here."

Julis scoffed. "You say that as if you actually ever considered letting me go in the first place."

Silas walked toward her without saying a word, then kicked her right in the wound on her thigh, hard. She screamed.

He laughed gleefully. "No, I was thinking of making you suffer a little first. But I've changed my mind. Let's finish this, shall we."

He turned his back to Julis as she twisted in agony, then lightly lifted his hand. As she stood pinned up against the wall, one of the dolls lifted up a giant battle-ax. Julis squeezed her eyes shut.

For an instant, a gust of wind stirred. Gentle, pleasant, and yet fierce...

"Sorry I'm late."

Hearing that voice, Julis opened her eyes to see a boy who was not supposed to be there. He held a greatsword of pure white.

"Ayato!?" As she yelled out in surprise, the doll with the battle-ax crumpled to the ground, and the ones that held her did the same. All of them had been sliced cleanly through the torso with a single swing of the sword.

"Wh-why are you here...?" Suddenly he was holding her up in his arms. She was relieved, but beyond that, a complicated mix of happy and embarrassed.

"All thanks to Saya and Claudia."

"Sasamiya and Claudia...?" Then she snapped, "Don't tell me you came here to save me!"

"Um, I kind of did?" he replied, flustered.

Now she was angry. He didn't even understand why she had to settle this on her own. She admitted it—she was fond of him, this flighty but kindhearted boy. And that was precisely the reason why she did not want him involved.

"This is my problem! It has nothing to do with you! But you just want to throw yourself into harm's way!?"

Ayato answered the question with a strangely calm expression on his face. "You told me the other day—you're fighting of your own free will, for yourself. You're trying to protect the children at the orphanage only because you want to."

"Yes…that's true." The sudden change of subject was bewildering, but she nodded.

"I think that's amazing, really I do, but…" Ayato looked straight into her eyes. "Who's going to protect *you*, Julis?"

"Protect…me?" She had never even thought about such a thing.

It was all she could do to not lose the things she had. To regain the things she had lost.

To take control of the future so that the past would not repeat itself…

"I've been searching, Julis. All this time. For something that I can do, something that I want to do, something I should do—for the thing that I have to do. Ever since the day someone I loved left me. But then I came here and met you. And now I finally know what that thing is."

Ayato sounded as if he were remembering something…and yet, at the same time, as if he were breaking away from it.

"I see it now. That if there's something I want to do, and I have the strength to do it—then that's it. What I have to do."

"What you…have to…?"

"Right now, I want to help you. That's all." Ayato nodded to her with a small smile.

He looked at Julis with such earnest, unwavering eyes. Deep and dark. Eyes like the night sky.

Her heart was pounding. A strange emotion welled up inside her—painful, agonizing, and at the same time comforting. Powerful, fierce, like nothing she had ever felt before…

"Are you done chatting now? You're quite the unexpected guest, Ayato Amagiri."

Recalled to the present, she saw Silas dramatically roll his shoulders. He was still brimming with arrogance, indifferent to the fact that Ayato had instantly destroyed three of the dolls. Apparently, he was confident that one new arrival would not change his advantage in this fight.

"So that's the power of the Ser Veresta… Yes, it might pose a *little* trouble."

Julis had heard of it—the Blade of the Black Furnace, famed as a sword of tremendous power, among the highest tier of Orga Luxes in the possession of Seidoukan Academy.

It was an enormous sword with a blinding white blade, but Ayato held it one-handed.

"What a waste. An Orga Lux in the hands of a second-class fighter. I've seen you fight several times, Ayato, and to be honest, at our school your skills are the very picture of mediocrity. You did well to ambush *those* three, but what do you hope to achieve against over one hundred—"

"Be quiet. You're the one who knows nothing but ambushing, Silas Norman."

Ayato's voice was low and cold, hardly like him at all.

Silas took a step backward as if overwhelmed by its force. Then, self-conscious of his loss of composure, he scowled.

"That's a bit harsh. Would you like to see what I can do?" As he snapped his fingers, his dolls all readied their Luxes. "You think you can take on this many dolls by yourself? Then let's see you try!"

Bullets of light flew from every direction, and between them lunged dolls with swords, axes, and spears. But a voice rang out—

"By the sword within me, I break free of this prison of stars and unchain my power!"

Then Julis saw it. Agony filled Ayato's face. As she sensed his prana heightening, glowing magic circles floated around him only to shatter in brilliant sparks. An overwhelming level of prana shot forth and rose in a pillar of pure light.

It was as if fetters holding him back had fallen...

In the next moment, Ayato was gone.

"Wuh...?"

As Silas uttered that stupefied syllable, his attacking dolls fell in pieces. They had been sliced apart as if by heat as much as by a blade, the sheared edges sizzling red.

"No! This is impossible!" Coming to, Silas looked around him in terror. "Where *are* you—!?"

"Right here."

Ayato was standing obliquely behind Silas, who yelped in dismay.

He had circled around in an instant, with Julis in one arm, and cut through the dolls with a single blow.

It looked as though a hurricane-force gust of wind had swept through the scene. What had happened, Julis knew, was that Ayato had moved at an otherworldly speed.

"*How...!?*" Silas turned in a panic, his face colorless, and began to back away as if preparing to flee.

In front of him stood a boy with a greatsword in his right hand and a girl in his left arm, cloaked in a profusion of prana so thick that it was visible to the naked eye.

"Wh-what are you...?" Silas stammered.

Julis was speechless with wonder, until she returned to her senses and immediately addressed Ayato. "Hey—put me down already! I refuse to be a burden!"

He could hardly fight unencumbered while carrying a person, she thought. On top of that, he was wielding the Ser Veresta one-handed, which, judging from the size of the sword, had to pose a significant burden in itself.

"No. If I leave you alone, then he'll be after you for sure. Sorry, but you'll have to put up with this a little while longer."

"But you can't fight with one arm...!"

"Don't worry about that. This thing is lighter than it looks," said Ayato and swung the Ser Veresta to demonstrate. The blade had been white as fresh snow, but now it was covered in black patterns—no, they were floating in the air, twining close around it.

Those strange patterns made Julis think of black flames escaping from the pit of hell. That must have been the truth behind the sword's epithet.

"Well, to be honest, I can't keep it up very long... But I can handle someone at his level." Ayato turned his eyes on Silas.

"You may be able to hold your own, but don't underestimate me!" Silas was making an effort to regain his composure, but they could see that he was clearly rattled. "I won't hold back this time..."

The dolls, lined up roughly in rows, now arranged themselves neatly into formation. The front ranks held long weapons such as spears and battle-axes, and the rear held guns and crossbows, while in between stood those with swords and hand axes. At the very back was Silas.

"This is the true spirit of my Maelzel Corps! They have the destructive power of a whole company of infantry! Defend yourself, if you can!"

The front rank of dolls mercilessly rushed in.

As Ayato leaped to dodge the numerous blades pointed at him, a hail of bullets of light followed. He deflected those with the flat of the Ser Veresta, but as he landed, more dolls jumped at him with swords. Ayato ducked underneath them and took a large step back, putting some distance in front of him.

Julis was finally able to breathe out.

The dolls had gotten close enough for sharp edges to graze their throats. She couldn't help but tighten her clutch around Ayato's neck, but each time she did, the fact of her clinging to him made her face warm. She admonished herself for thinking that way at a time like this—but there was nothing for it.

Silas broke into jeering laughter. Seeing Ayato on the defensive had restored his arrogance. "You're very good at dodging. Are you going to do something besides running from them?"

"Maybe. I learned a lot just now."

"You learned something?"

"You can only move about six types of dolls at the same time. Isn't that right?"

"Huh?" Perplexed, Silas frowned. "What are you talking about now? Are you even looking at them? Can't you see that I'm controlling over one hundred—?"

"Sure, I see that. But there are only six types moving freely, and the rest just follow simple patterns. And I think you can control around sixteen individual dolls at once. The rest of them just repeat simple motions like pulling triggers and swinging their arms."

Silas said nothing to this.

"It might be useful as a bluff, but now I see why you can only fight with sneak attacks. If you participated in a regular fight, it wouldn't take very long for people to see through your lousy ability."

Silas trembled as the color drained from his face, confirming Ayato's statements.

"Oh, six types and sixteen dolls. Are you Imaging a game of chess?"

"Chess—! I see!" Julis exclaimed.

Dantes and Stregas controlled their powers by conjuring specific images in their minds. Just as Julis Imaged flowers, Silas must be Imaging chess pieces.

This all made sense to Julis, but she was in awe of Ayato's perception. If he really had deduced all of that in just a few moments of combat, then his abilities were far beyond what the likes of Silas could handle.

"You might think you're quite the grand master," Ayato went on, "but I'd say you're a pretty mediocre player."

"Damn yooooouuuuu!" In a full reversal, Silas flushed dark red and howled in rage. "*Crush* them! Crush them dead!"

The front ranks of dolls rushed at him again, but this time Ayato did not even bother to dodge them. He walked toward the swarming dolls and casually swung the greatsword. That was enough to slice in half three dolls with spears in their hands. His blade had moved at an extraordinary speed. He looked as if he were waving away gnats, but the dolls fell, several at a time.

"It's no use. Taken one by one, your dolls aren't very strong. And once I've figured out how they move, they're as flimsy as marionettes." Ayato thrust out his sword without looking, and one of the dolls jumped to impale itself as if of its own free will. With a sizzling sound, it melted to the ground. He had a complete grasp of their movements.

"So…let's finish this already."

The moment those words left him, Ayato jumped into the horde of dolls. With each flash of his blade, there were fewer left standing. Some of the dolls made as if to defend themselves, but to no avail. The Ser Veresta was so immensely powerful that ordinary Luxes could not even parry its blows. It simply cut through any other blades of light that tried to halt its path.

The dolls that were trying to shoot at Ayato from behind pillars and rubble melted like butter along with their cover of debris.

Julis couldn't suppress a shudder of horror at that overwhelming power. *A sword against which there is no defense…?* Even for an Orga Lux, this was absurd. And Ayato's attacks were too fast to dodge.

In less than three minutes, it was over. Every last one of Silas's dolls, over one hundred in number, had been slain. The heavyweight models built for Lester, the heat-resistant ones built for Julis—they all lay halved on the ground.

"It can't be… This can't be happening. It just can't…" Silas looked on the scene as if completely petrified, but then screamed and fell on his posterior as Ayato trained the Ser Veresta on him.

"The game is over, Silas."

"Not yet! I still have a piece left!" Although still without his balance, Silas waved his arms wildly.

The pile of rubble behind him blew apart, and from it an enormous shadow emerged.

It must have been five times the size of the other dolls. Its head would have smashed through the ceiling if there were not already a hole in it. Its arms and legs were as thick as the pillars. It was humanoid, barely—more like a gorilla.

"Go, my queen!" Silas cackled. "Get him!"

At his command, the giant doll rushed at Ayato with a speed unbefitting its huge stature. It held no weapons, presumably because it needed none. An attack from such massive limbs would crush even Genestella.

Ayato sighed and readied the Ser Veresta again. In the very moment that the doll raised its fists to mash them to death, the sword flashed.

"Rend the five viscera and sever the four limbs. Amagiri Shinmei Style Middle Technique—*Nine-Fanged Blade!*"

Despite her close-up view, Julis had no idea what Ayato did. The Ser Veresta flashed briefly and then the giant doll fell to the ground with a crash, its arms and legs cut off. Large chunks of its torso had been carved through, but she hadn't glimpsed the kind of attack that could leave such damage. She couldn't even say how many times Ayato had swung his sword.

Silas sat, utterly unable to speak.

As Ayato approached him, he scrambled to flee, his face contorted in terror. He squealed, almost sobbing, aimlessly tumbling between the remains of his dolls.

"You really don't know when to give up." Ayato frowned in mock exasperation, then his expression turned serious.

He was about to make a move, but Silas was one step ahead. Silas clung onto the remains of a doll and floated into the air. Technically, it was the piece of a doll's body floating, but that amounted to the same thing. It accelerated upward with Silas and flew through the hole in the ceiling.

"Sorry, Julis. Can you wait here while I chase him down?"

"Fine with me, but can you catch him?"

"I think it's going to be close." Silas was already near the top floor. There was no telling what kind of trouble he would cause if he got away, Ayato thought.

"Then this is a job for me," said Julis.

"Huh…?"

"I told you before. I refuse to be a burden!"

Julis smiled dauntlessly and focused her prana.

"Burst into bloom—*Strelitzia!*"

Mana gathered onto Ayato and numerous pairs of fiery wings sprouted from his back. He cried out in surprise.

"Let's get moving!" said Julis. "I'll steer. Now give that sneaky little prick a good wallop!"

"That's…definitely not something a princess would say."

She ignored Ayato's quip and made the wings flap in one grand motion, lifting from the floor like a rocket. They shot up through the hole in the ceiling out into the dusky sky.

Julis had never flown the weight of two people before, but she had no misgivings. She could feel the strength welling up from inside her.

Accelerating even faster, they overtook Silas in a breath, then turned around to face him.

Ayato pointed his sword toward the master of dolls, who stared at them in disbelief. "It's checkmate for sure this time, Silas Norman."

"No, don't—*nooooooo!*"

They flew past him with a single flash of the sword. The doll piece shattered, and Silas plummeted down into an alley between abandoned buildings, leaving only the echo of a scream.

Silas was a Genestella. The fall would not kill him.

"Claudia and her team should be waiting for him down there," said Ayato. "Should we leave the rest to them?"

"That sounds good." Julis closed her eyes and breathed in deeply. A lot had happened, but their work was done for now. The wind that buffeted them felt pleasant on her skin.

"What a view...," he murmured.

She opened her eyes again. "Oh, it is a beautiful view."

The city was painted red in the setting sun. The streets, the sky, the lake—all crimson.

As the wings of fire flapped above them, Julis and Ayato exchanged smiles in the sky.

Suddenly he made a muffled cry, his face twisted in pain.

"What's wrong?" Julis asked him, startled, but before he answered, she could feel something strange happening.

The mana around them was being sucked into Ayato—by extraordinary amounts.

"Wh-what's going on...?" There was no hint of a Strega or Dante nearby.

Which meant that this could have been prepared in advance. Such a thing was not rare. There were many abilities that could be activated after a time lapse or only when certain conditions were met.

But what on earth could someone be doing with this much mana...?

Ayato screamed as magic circles surrounded him. Chains of light shot out from them, then coiled themselves around him—binding him.

"It's the same...!" These were just like the magic circles that had emerged earlier, when his prana had risen so intensely.

Then all this is to suppress his powers? Such a tremendous amount of mana, just for that…!?

She heard him groan. "H-hey! Ayato, hang on! Ayato!"

But his body went limp as he fainted.

Luckily for them, Julis was the one controlling the wings of fire. But it was no longer safe to be this high in the air. For one thing, Ayato had been holding her up earlier, and now she had to cling to him with all her might.

"*Argh!* I can't believe this!"

Julis flapped the wings and looked for a place to land nearby.

*

"I'm sorry, Ayato." Smiling, and yet on the verge of tears, the girl placed her hand softly on his head.

"Haruka…?" The boy in his threadbare student robe looked back at her in confusion.

It was just the two of them in the moonlit dojo, nothing else in that hollow space but the hushed chirping of insects and the clinging night air.

That night, there was something different about her.

Her kind and gentle bearing, her regal voice—those were the same as ever. Still, the boy sensed something unusual in the way she looked at him.

Just as he opened his mouth to ask her, she closed her eyes as if to stop him.

"I'm sorry." As the girl repeated those words, a terrible impact rushed at him, as jarring as if sky and earth had reversed.

A shriek tore from his throat. Violent shocks of pain ran through his body as if he was being electrocuted. He could not even writhe in agony, suddenly bound by countless punishing chains that had emerged from thin air. When he managed to look up, he was able to see myriad intricate symbols, like magic circles, swirling around his sister's raised hand.

The boy did not know why this was happening.

No—he did. He knew. This was her ability: the forbidden power to seal off the flow of nature and restrain anything and everything. The infernal power of a Strega.

But the girl hated her powers, and there was nothing in the world that would make her turn them on *him*. Or so he had believed.

"H-Haruka… Why…?" His voice was weak and hoarse. The strength drained from the depths of his body.

Her eyes still closed, the girl murmured solemnly:

"With these fetters do I confine thy power."

And then everything vanished, as if his very senses had snapped apart. It was like plunging into a bottomless swamp. The world sank mercilessly into darkness. In that hazy state, his consciousness fading, he knew nothing but the girl's subdued voice ringing inside his skull.

"Remember what I told you years ago? I said that I would protect you. That's why…"

Even that voice faded, and he reached out, desperate for something to hold on to.

"But I don't want this! I said *I* would protect *you*—!" He had been training so hard for that reason—*only* for that. But now—

"Good-bye, Ayato. I love you."

Those were the last of her words that he remembered.

When he opened his eyes, he saw Julis's face right in front of his, looking worried.

She brightened as soon as she noticed that his eyes were open. "Good, you're finally awake. I was starting to wonder."

"Um, where are— Ow!" Before his awareness fully returned, Ayato tried to get up and winced at a jolt of pain. That made him remember what had happened. "Oh. So I did faint."

"Don't overexert yourself. We're on the roof of that abandoned building. I sent a message to Claudia, so people will come for us any minute now."

"Thanks. I think I'll need the help." In fact, he doubted he would be able to walk for a little while.

He idly looked around to see that the sun must have long since set. A sky full of stars spread out above them.

"I—I don't want your thanks. You're the one who saved me." With that, Julis curtly turned away.

Her usual brand of sincerity. Somehow it made Ayato glad.

He was gazing at her when it suddenly occurred to him that something was not quite right.

His head was resting on something too soft to be the bare roof. He could smell a faint floral aroma.

"H-hey! Don't move so much!"

And her face was so close… Ayato had been lying with his head on Julis's thighs all this time.

"Gah! S-sorry! I'll get off—*nngh*!" Alarmed, he tried to heave himself up, only for pain to shoot through him again like lightning.

"It's fine. Just keep still, you idiot! It obviously hurts to move, so don't move!"

"B-but—"

"I say it's fine, so it is! Deal with it!" Julis turned away again, now so red that it looked like she might spontaneously combust. She smacked him lightly on the forehead.

"Uh—okay." There was nothing he could do but give her a tiny nod of acquiescence, his face also flushed red.

She cleared her throat and glared down at him from the corner of her eyes. "More importantly, are you going to give me an explanation?"

"Um, explanation for what…?"

"Oh, let's start with that power holding you back—it must be a Strega or a Dante. Who did this to you?"

"Um, well, it…" Ayato avoided looking at her and tried to come up with something, but as Julis brought her face closer to his, he let out a resigned sigh. "It was my sister. Her ability is the power of imprisonment, to chain and confine all things."

Her expression darkened as she took this in. "Hmm… So, what I just saw was your true strength?"

"You could say that. But you could also say that it's not."

"What does that mean?" she retorted, annoyed. "That's not a very satisfying answer."

Ayato smiled bitterly. "Isn't it weird to call it my 'true strength,' when I can hardly control it?"

"It looked to me like you could control it just fine."

"For a limited amount of time, that's true. But this was the first time I lasted more than five minutes. And after that, I'm like this for a while, I can't even move. It's not exactly something to brag about." The first time he'd unleashed his strength, he lasted only ten seconds.

"Why would your sister do this to you?"

"I'd like to ask her that myself. But she went missing five years ago."

Julis bit her tongue, looking as if she regretted the question.

Ayato waved it away. "It's okay, though. I think she had her reasons. There must be some meaning to what she did. Oh, can I ask you something, too?"

"Hmm? What is it?"

"Do you have a partner for the Phoenix yet?"

She flinched, making a tiny sound of chagrin, which was enough of a reply.

Ayato sighed in relief. "Um…how about me?"

"What?"

"My integrity isn't impeccable, but it's not too spotty, either. And I'm no worse than average at thinking on my feet, I think. As for a strong will and noble spirit, you might have to let those slide…"

"So…you want me to compromise on all of my standards?" Julis gave him a small astounded smile. "I appreciate the offer. But don't put yourself through that. You won't be able to fight in the Festa at your usual strength, and I'd rather not watch this happen to you after every match."

"Oh, I don't mind at all," Ayato said bluntly. "I told you. The thing I have to do—it's to help you, Julis."

A blush began to color her cheeks. "But, you see, really, you can't just…"

"Are you embarrassed? Your face is bright red."

"Shut up! I am not! And stop looking at me!" She smacked him lightly again.

It didn't hurt, but this time she kept her hand there, covering his eyes.

They were silent for a moment.

"Julis…?" Ayato tried, but there was no reply. Instead, he felt a hint of tension come into the hand that rested on his face.

"Do you…really mean it?" she said in a low, trembling voice.

Her usual tone brimmed with confidence. This was entirely different. It was a voice filled with uncertainty, frail to the point of breaking. The voice of someone who was afraid of holding out her hand to someone and of accepting a hand held out to her.

But that's totally normal, Ayato thought. Anyone would be afraid, stepping out onto a new path. It was only natural.

And maybe this was the real Julis—a normal, perfectly ordinary girl. But here she was, an ordinary girl, trying so dauntlessly and nobly to live true to her own convictions. Wasn't that admirable? Wasn't it beautiful?

So Ayato gave her the clearest answer he could. "Of course I do."

I won't regret this. And I'm going to make sure she doesn't, either. Not this time.

"You really are an odd one," said Julis.

Her hand lifted from his face, and he saw her smiling against the sky of glittering stars.

Their light caught in a droplet at the corner of her eye. He reached up without a word and softly wiped it away.

EPILOGUE

Silas Norman dragged himself desperately through the back alleys of the redevelopment area.

He had managed to break his fall by gathering the remains of his dolls into a sort of cushion, but of course that did little to actually prevent injury. He did not know how many bones he had broken, but there was plenty of pain, shooting through his body like lightning.

Still, he could not slow down.

He knew they were looking for him—Shadowstar, the special operations unit under the direct command of Seidoukan Academy's integrated enterprise foundation. No matter what it took, he must not let himself be captured. They would use any and all means necessary to extract all the information he had. And after that…

"Damn it! Why won't they pick up!?"

He had to get himself into Allekant's protective custody as soon as possible, but the mobile device he had for the purpose of contacting them was of no avail.

"If I'm captured, they'll be in trouble, too…!" he spat.

"Aren't you overestimating your own value a little bit, Mr. Norman?"

Silas yelped in surprise as a golden-haired girl stepped from the darkness to block his path.

"P-president…!"

In each hand she held an eerie-looking sword. The motif on the guards resembled eyeballs, and when held out as a pair, the swords called to mind the eyes of a terrible monster.

It was the Orga Lux Pan-Dora. Silas had never seen the notorious weapon in person, but rumors of its power had reached him.

"Poor boy," said Claudia. "To them you were no more than a pawn to be sacrificed."

"How about a deal, Miss Enfield?" he said in a rush.

"A deal? With me?"

"Everything—I'll tell you everything I know! And in exchange, I want you to guarantee my safety! Hand me over to the disciplinary committee and not Shadowstar!"

She cocked her head. "And why should I do that?" she asked curtly.

Silas gloated to himself. *I still have a chance if she's willing to negotiate.*

"Shadowstar would get rid of me in total secrecy," he explained. "But if the disciplinary committee got involved, all of this would have to be public record. Then you could use me as a chip against Allekant...!"

"Hmm..." Claudia closed her eyes in thought.

Taking that as a good sign, he went on. "We're alike, you and I. We think of others only as pieces in a game. The fools around us might criticize us for it, but using the pieces you have to their highest advantage is simply how you win the game. I know you understand that!"

"I see... You do have a point."

Silas's expression brightened at her words. *I knew this Claudia was a pragmatic girl. That sort of cleverness is so easy to manipulate.*

Claudia, however, smiled sweetly. "But there *is* one big difference between you and me, Mr. Norman."

"Huh...?"

"You seem to fancy yourself the player in control of the pieces, but I think of myself as a piece, too. The game isn't any fun otherwise, in my opinion." She let out a giggle as if she really were enjoying herself. "Now, I could publicize this case for some political leverage, but it's more beneficial for me to deal with it secretly and let Allekant owe me one."

His face twitched and his knees shook. With a long, furious howl, Silas used his last trump card. He drew the knife hidden in his clothes and hurled it at Claudia. She could not dodge it from this distance. The timing was perfect, he thought, completely self-assured.

"Oh, dear—surely you must know about my little one's power."

Claudia sent the knife flying with her blade *as if she'd already known the attack was coming*. It was no use.

As he was about to take a step back, the knife embedded itself into the ground at his feet. Silas cried out in fear.

"There's no need to be afraid. You're still of some value to me. For the time being, anyway." Claudia wore her usual smile, but her gaze was icy, detached.

Silas couldn't move.

"Farewell," she said in a clear voice, and the twin swords danced.

Silas saw an uncanny glint in the eyes on the hand guards, just as blood began to spurt from all over his body.

"So this…this is the Pan-Dora…"

His knees buckled and he collapsed on the spot.

It was a pair of magic swords that granted the power of foresight—one of the most potent Orga Luxes in the possession of Seidoukan Academy.

Silas's school crest snapped into pieces. As his consciousness faded, he felt someone approach.

"Oh, man. You didn't kill him, did you?"

The boy, who seemed to seep out from the shadows behind a streetlamp, spoke to Claudia in a cheery tone that was rather out of place with what he'd just witnessed.

"Don't worry. You can toss him into a holding cell for a bit. I'll leave the rest to you at Shadowstar, but please be sure to get out what information he has."

"But of course. That *is* our job, after all." The boy looked at Silas lying on the ground and shrugged, barely interested. "What happened with the other two?"

"I just heard from Julis. Everything went well."

"But you don't look too happy about it."

"Oops… I guess I'll have to work on my poker face, if you can tell."

"If you were going to regret it so much, why didn't you go with them?" the boy asked, exasperated.

"Things aren't so simple. I have the duties of my office to uphold."

"Oh, is that it?" He smirked.

Without the hint of a break in her smile, Claudia thrust the point of a blade in front of his eyes. "Do you have orders to look into my affairs, Eishirou Yabuki?"

"No! None at all!" The boy shook his head in panicked denial, but there was something clownish in his mannerisms. "I was speaking out of pure curiosity. I just wondered if it was right to leave everything to them, that's all."

Claudia let her shoulders fall. "Well, there's nothing for it now," she murmured with a sigh. "I'll let Julis have this one. The main event is just beginning."

*

Absorbing the report in a dimly lit laboratory, the girl rested her hands for a moment and let out a tiny sigh.

"Well, I guess it's time to pull out. I got plenty of data, and he actually did a good job ambushing all those students."

She had countless air-windows open around her, displaying a constantly changing array of numbers and plots.

"Oh, but maybe that's just because my pretty dolls were so good!" She laughed aloud in high spirits and pulled up an optical keyboard. "I like the halfway-clever ones—so easy to manipulate!"

With an indomitable smile on her lips, she continued her work.

Her industrious gaze focused on two dolls in quiet slumber.

AFTERWORD
FROM THE AUTHOR

Hello, everyone. I'm Yuu Miyazaki. I'm just a novice, so this is my first serialized volume, but it's good to meet you all.

I hope that you liked *The Asterisk War: Encounter with a Fiery Princess.*

As you can tell from the title, it's a story from the "school battle" genre.

In a world changed by a mysterious disaster called the Invertia, students from six schools vie for supremacy to make their dreams come true—well, that's the plan, anyway. In this volume, you only see the school where the main characters go.

And yet, even with just one school, there are so many intertwining characters with their own circumstances—and I'm talking about doing six schools. It seems like I might have bitten off more than I can chew. I almost want to tell myself to be more cautious and write something more in line with my abilities.

But now that the story has gotten started, no excuses! I'm going to do all that I can to chew what I've bitten, so I hope that you decide to join me for the ride.

Incidentally, I'm one of those people who loves tabletop RPGs, but my favorite part is reading about the worldbuilding in the rule books. You know, things like "Here are the legends about the gods worshipped in this region and their devotees follow these precepts" or "In this country, the such-and-such industries are flourishing, and their customs are like this." Just these tiny pieces of information, but it really sets your imagination flying.

In tabletop RPGs, the players have total freedom to make their own story. That means that there has to be a foundation from which to build a story, no matter which parts of the worldbuilding the players focus on and how they interpret them. You could call this detailed information the seeds of a story. Of course, the players have the right to build their story while paying as little attention as they want to those seeds. But personally, I prefer worldbuilding where there are as many of those seeds as possible.

That's the kind of worldbuilding I hope to establish in *The Asterisk War*. Ayato is the protagonist, but there are many other students living in this city.

The illustrator for this volume is okiura. I remember being just amazed at his first rough sketch of Julis. "Awesome!" I yelled.

I'm truly indebted to him, because this is a story that places a large burden on the illustrator. He has the task of designing the uniforms, crests, characters, and weapons for all six schools, which really adds up to six times the usual amount of work. I'm so, so grateful to him.

In particular, for a majority of the Luxes and Orga Luxes, I incorporated aspects of okiura's designs into my writing. He's contributed lots of other ideas, too, and I can't thank him enough.

Many, many people have helped me since this project started.

First and foremost, my editor, Iwaasa. I want to thank him for his countless pieces of great advice, from the detailed settings to the backstories of the characters. Without him, this story would never have seen the light of day. (He was also the one who suggested including the map of the city and the glossary!)

I also want to thank Shimizu and Shouji of the editorial staff. And Okada, who gave me the first words of advice—it's thanks to her that this story has settled on its current trajectory!

*   *   *

I also want to thank the chief editor Misaka and everyone else who is involved. And above all, from the bottom of my heart, I'd like to thank you, the readers who picked up this book.

I look forward to seeing you all in the next volume.

Yuu Miyazaki
August 2012

-Afterword-

Hello.

I'm okiura, the illustrator for
The Asterisk War.

When I first read the novel,
I was completely pulled in
by Mr. Miyazaki's wonderfully
descriptive prose. I hope all the
readers feel it, too. And I hope
that my illustrations can help add
to its charm.

Please keep looking forward to
the adventures of Ayato, the
heroines, and all the schools!

THE WORLD OF
THE ASTERISK WAR
GLOSSARY

THE INVERTIA

A mysterious disaster that befell Earth in the twentieth century. Meteors fell all over the world for three days and three nights, destroying many cities. As a result, the strength of existing nations declined considerably, and a new form of economic power known as "integrated enterprise foundations" took their place.

A previously unknown element called *mana* was extracted from the meteorites, leading to advances in scientific technology as well as a new type of human with extraordinary powers, called Genestella.

The Invertia was undetected by all the observatories in the world, and the destruction it caused was actually much less than ordinary meteors, so the pervading theory is that it did not consist of normal meteors.

INTEGRATED ENTERPRISE FOUNDATION

A new type of economic entity formed by corporations that merged to overcome the choatic economic situation following the Invertia. Their power far surpasses that of the diminished nations.

There used to be eight IEFs, but there are currently six: Galaxy, EP (Elliott-Pound), Jie Long, Solnage, Frauenlob, and W&W (Warren & Warren). They vie for advantage over one another and effectively control the world. Each one sponsors an academy in Asterisk.

THE FESTA

A fighting tournament where students compete, held in Asterisk, and operated by the IEFs. Each cycle, or "season," consists of three events: the tag match (Phoenix) in the summer of the first year, the team battle (Gryps) in the fall of the second year, and the individual match (Lindvolus) in the winter of the third year. Victory is achieved by destroying the opponent's school crest, and the rules are set forth in the Stella Carta. As the event is held for entertainment, acts of deliberate cruelty and attacks intended to cause death or injury can be penalized.

The event is the most popular one in the world, with matches broadcast internationally. The IEFs prioritize economic success and growth above all else, so the direction of the Festa has always been driven by the majority demand of consumers. (This is why the fighters are students—viewers want to see beautiful boys and girls fight one another.) Some speak out against the Festa on ethical grounds, but under the rule of the IEFs, those voices have fallen from justified dissent to unpopular opinion.

The cultures of the different schools veer to extremes, which is also by design, for the sake of the Festa.

THE STELLA CARTA

Rules that apply strictly to all the students of Asterisk. Those who violate these rules are harshly penalized, sometimes by expulsion. If a school is found to have been involved, the administration can also be subject to penalty. The Stella Carta has been amended several times in the past. The most important items are as follows:

- Combat between students of Asterisk is permitted only insofar as the intent is to destroy the other's school crest.
- Each student of Asterisk shall be eligible to participate in the Festa between the ages of 13 and 22, a period spanning ten years.
- Each student of Asterisk shall participate in the Festa no more than three times.

Ⓜ️ANA

A previously unknown element that was brought to Earth by the Invertia. By now, it can be found all over the world. It responds to the will of living beings who meet certain criteria, incorporating surrounding elements to form objects and create phenomena.

Ⓖ️ENESTELLA

A new type of human being, born after regular human children were exposed to mana. With an aura known as *prana*, they possess physical abilities far beyond those of ordinary humans. Genestella who can tap into mana without special equipment are called Stregas (female) and Dantes (male).

Discrimination against Genestella is a pervasive social problem, and many students come to Asterisk to escape this. (The negative bias against Genestella is one reason why opposition to the Festa is in the minority.)

Ⓟ️RANA

A kind of aura unique to Genestella. Stregas and Dantes deplete prana as they use their powers. They lose consciousness if they run out of prana, but it can simply be replenished with time. The manipulation of prana is a basic skill among Genestella, and by focusing it, they can increase offensive or defensive strength. This is especially effective for defense, which explains why serious injuries among Asterisk students are rare despite the common use of weapons.

Ⓜ️ETEORIC ENGINEERING

A field of science that studies mana and the meteorites from the Invertia. Many mysteries remain pertaining to mana, but experimentation on manadite has advanced significantly. Fueled by the abundance of rare metals found in the meteorites, manadite research has yielded a large variety of practical applications.

Ⓜ️ANADITE

A special ore made of crystallized mana. If stress is applied, it can store or retain specific elemental patterns. Before the Invertia, it did not exist on Earth, and it must be extracted from meteorites. Manadite is used in Lux activators, as well as manufactured products developed through meteoric engineering.

Ⓛ️UX

A type of weapon with a manadite core. Records of elemental patterns are stored in pieces of manadite and re-created using activators. By gathering mana from the surroundings, they can create blades or projectiles of light. Mana also acts as the energy source for Lux weapons.

Ⓤ️RM-MANADITE

A name for exceptionally pure manadite, much rarer than ordinary manadite. Luxes using urm-manadite are known as Orga Luxes. Urm-manadite crystals come in myriad colors and shapes, and no two are the same. They are said to have minds of their own.

Ⓞ️RGA LUX

A weapon using urm-manadite as its core. Many of them have special powers, but using them takes a toll—a certain "cost." The weapons themselves have something akin to a sentient will, and unsuitable users cannot even touch the weapon. Suitability is measured by means of a compatibility rating.

Most Orga Luxes are owned by the IEFs and are entrusted to the schools of Asterisk for the purpose of lending them to students with high compatibility ratings.

WATCH ON crunchyroll

www.crunchyroll.com/the-asterisk-war

THE AsteriskWar

©2015 Yuu Miyazaki, PUBLISHED BY KADOKAWA CORPORATION / Asterisk Projec

THE ASTERISK WAR

Please flip to the end of the book to read a special preview of the manga adaptation of THE ASTERISK WAR!

—ARE STREGA!

HUH.

SO YOU MANAGED TO DODGE THAT?

THERE ARE SPECIAL CLASSES EVEN WITHIN THE GENES TELLA...

THOSE FEW WITH THE POWER TO BEND THE LAWS OF NATURE BY LINKING THEMSELVES WITH MANA, LIKE HER—

NOT BAD.

TON (TMP)

I'LL GIVE YOU A REAL FIGHT, FOR A BIT.

VERY WELL, THEN.

BOO

...YOU MEAN, YOU WANT TO COOK ME ALL THE WAY THROUGH?

WHAT NOW?

HOLD ON, OKAY!?

WHO—

JUST DON'T GIVE ME ANY MORE TROUBLE, AND I'LL BE NICE AND TURN OFF THE GRILL WHEN YOU'RE WELL-DONE.

READ MORE IN *THE ASTERISK WAR* MANGA VOLUME 1, IN STORES NOW!

UH, I'M GLAD YOU GOT IT BACK.

AH HA HA...

ALL THE SAME.

I REALLY DO APPRECIATE IT!

I MEAN, I JUST HAPPENED TO FIND IT...

OH, NO —

ASE
(FLUSTER)
あせ

ASE

OH—YOU DON'T HAVE TO THANK ME THAT MUCH—

I MEAN, ALL I DID WAS PICK IT UP, SO...

PEKORI
(BOW)
ペコリ

YES, ME TOO...

...WELL...

THAT'S SETTLED, I'D SAY.

...UH?

ZAKU
(RAGE)

THEN —

BA (SWING)

PASHI (GRAB)

FUWA (FLOAT)

TAN (LEAP)

UM...

PAA (GLOW)

SORRY FOR BARGING IN LIKE THIS...

...BUT DID YOU HAPPEN TO DROP A HAND-KERCHIEF...?

MADE IT!

TON (TMP)

THE FOURTH FLOOR...

...SO THAT'S IT.

ANYWAY!

—I HAVE TO CHASE IT DOWN BEFORE IT FLIES AWAY ANY FARTHER!

GOGO
(RUMMAGED)

...SO IT SHOULDN'T BE TOO HARD.

HM...

THERE ARE SOME FOOT-HOLDS...

WELL...

HERE GOES...!

ZAAAAA
(RUSTLE)

FLOATING ON THE SURFACE OF A VAST CRATER LAKE...

—BETTER KNOWN AS ASTERISK.

...IS A CITY CALLED RIKKA.

I'M A LITTLE EARLY...

THE GREATEST FIGHTING SHOW IN THE WORLD, THE FESTA, TAKES PLACE HERE.

IT IS ALSO AN ACADEMIC CITY, WHERE GENESTELLA FROM ALL OVER THE WORLD COME TO STUDY.

THE ASTERISK WAR 01

Ningen
Original Story: Yuu Miyazaki
Character Design: okiura

Translation: Melissa Tanaka   Lettering: Morgan Hart

This book is a work of fiction. Names, characters, places, and incidents are the product of the author's imagination or are used fictitiously. Any resemblance to actual events, locales, or persons, living or dead, is coincidental.

THE ASTERISK WAR
© Ningen 2014
© Yuu Miyazaki 2014
First published in Japan in 2014 by KADOKAWA CORPORATION, Tokyo.
English translation rights arranged with KADOKAWA CORPORATION, Tokyo, through TUTTLE-MORI AGENCY, Inc., Tokyo.

English translation © 2016 by Yen Press, LLC

Yen Press, LLC supports the right to free expression and the value of copyright. The purpose of copyright is to encourage writers and artists to produce the creative works that enrich our culture.

The scanning, uploading, and distribution of this book without permission is a theft of the author's intellectual property. If you would like permission to use material from the book (other than for review purposes), please contact the publisher. Thank you for your support of the author's rights.

Yen Press
1290 Avenue of the Americas
New York, NY 10104

Visit us at yenpress.com
facebook.com/yenpress
twitter.com/yenpress
yenpress.tumblr.com

First Yen Press Edition: July 2016

Yen Press is an imprint of Yen Press, LLC.
The Yen Press name and logo are trademarks of Yen Press, LLC.

The publisher is not responsible for websites (or their content) that are not owned by the publisher.

BVG

Printed in the United States of America

THE ASTERISK WAR

01

ART: **Ningen**
ORIGINAL STORY: **Yuu Miyazaki**
CHARACTER DESIGN: **okiura**